## PRAISE FOR *DEAD TO* ...

"McMann's narrative is layered and emotional, with constant questions about family dynamics, identity, and reconciliation. While an amnesia-based plot risks a quick foray into formula, this resists, balancing the fractured nature of Ethan's recollections nicely with the character's development. The sibling rivalry builds secondary tension and suspense."

—*Kirkus Reviews*

"The bitter cold of a Minnesota winter serves as both metaphor and backdrop for a riveting read that is like the dark side of Caroline B. Cooney's *The Face on the Milk Carton*. A realistic but shocking ending makes this an excellent choice for book discussion, and the simple sentence structure and complex content will appeal to reluctant readers."

—Booklist

"The dynamics are credible and compelling, and Ethan's challenge in negotiating the complicated territory will ring true. . . ."

—BCCB

"Ethan's first-person story . . . successfully explores the emotional devastation on those closest to an abducted child and a child's ability to cope with trauma. The long-awaited but abrupt conclusion to the story's central mystery is dramatic, packing an emotional punch."

—SLJ

# DEAD TO YOU

LISA McMANN

**SIMON PULSE**

NEW YORK   LONDON   TORONTO   SYDNEY   NEW DELHI

SIMON PULSE

An imprint of Simon & Schuster Children's Publishing Division
1230 Avenue of the Americas, New York, NY 10020
First Simon Pulse paperback edition December 2012
Copyright © 2012 by Lisa McMann
All rights reserved, including the right of reproduction
in whole or in part in any form.
SIMON PULSE and colophon are registered trademarks
of Simon & Schuster, Inc.
Also available in a Simon Pulse hardcover edition.
For information about special discounts for bulk purchases, please contact
Simon & Schuster Special Sales at 1-866-506-1949
or business@simonandschuster.com.
The Simon & Schuster Speakers Bureau can bring authors to your live event.
For more information or to book an event contact the Simon & Schuster Speakers
Bureau at 1-866-248-3049 or visit our website at www.simonspeakers.com.
Designed by Mike Rosamilia
The text of this book was set in Janson Text.
Manufactured in the United States of America
2 4 6 8 10 9 7 5 3 1
The Library of Congress has cataloged the hardcover edition as follows:
McMann, Lisa.
Dead to you / by Lisa McMann.
p. cm.
Summary: Having been abducted at age seven, abandoned, a foster child,
and homeless, Ethan, now sixteen, is happy to be home until his brother's
suspicion and his own inability to remember something unspeakable
from his early childhood begin to tear the family apart.
[1. Family problems—Fiction. 2. Identity—Fiction.
3. Family life—Minnesota—Fiction. 4. Memory—Fiction.
5. Kidnapping—Fiction. 6. Minnesota—Fiction.] I. Title.
PZ7.M478757De 2012    [Fic] —dc23    2011034068
ISBN 978-1-4424-0388-8 (hc)
ISBN 978-1-4424-0389-5 (pbk)
ISBN 978-1-4424-0390-1 (eBook)

*For MB*

# ACKNOWLEDGMENTS

Many thanks to my amazing husband, Matt, for doing everything in the history and future of the universe so I can traipse around the country and write books and books and more books—you are AWESOME and I love you.

Thank you to my fantastic editor, Jennifer Klonsky, for believing in this book; to Michael Bourret for knowing me so well and sending me the article that inspired this story; and to my early readers, Kilian McMann, Kennedy McMann, Joanne Levy, Bethany Harowitz, and Barry Lyga for the early critiques. Thanks to the National Center for Missing and Exploited Children for the information provided. Any procedural inaccuracies or errors in the story are mine due to incompetence or artistic license. And thanks also to Michele Thomas of the Minneapolis Public School System for the answers about school procedure.

Most of all, thank *you*, dear reader, dear bookseller, dear librarian, dear teacher, dear parent, for supporting this book. I am grateful.

# DEAD TO YOU

# CHAPTER 1

There are three of them. No, four.

They step off the Amtrak train into the snowy dusk, children first and adults after, and then they hesitate, clustered on the platform. Passengers behind them shove past, but the four—Blake, Gracie, Dad, Mama—just move a few more steps and stop again, look around. Their faces are an uneasy yellow in the overhead light from the station. Mama looks most anxious. She peers into the darkness under the awning where I stand, just twenty feet away, as if she knows instinctively that I am here, but no confirmation registers on her face. I am still invisible in the shadows.

Invisible, but cornered. Backed up against the station wall, next to a bench, the woman from Child Protective

Services who I met this afternoon standing beside me. It's too late to stop this now. Too late to go back, too late to run away. I press my back into the wall, feeling the tenderness of a recent bruise on my right shoulder blade. I wet my chapped lips and break into a cold sweat.

"Is that them?" the woman asks quietly.

"It's them," I say. And I'm sure. I feel panic welling up in my gut.

If I move, they'll see me.

# CHAPTER 2

I take a deep breath, hold it, and force myself to step out from under the awning into the yellow light. Walk toward them. Mama sees me, and her mittened hand clutches her coat where it opens at her neck. As I approach, I can see her eyes shining above deep gray semicircles, and I can tell she's not sure—I'm not seven anymore. Her lips part and I imagine she gasps a bit. Then Dad, Blake, and finally Gracie, the replacement child, stare with doubting eyes, taking me in.

I open my mouth to say something, but I don't know what to say. It's almost like the cold sweat in the small of my back, in my armpits, freezes me in place.

Mama takes Dad's arm and they stumble over to me while the two children hang back. And then they're right in front of me, and I'm looking into Mama's eyes.

"Ethan?" she says within a visible exhaled breath that envelopes me, then dissipates. She touches my hair, my cheek. Her breath smells like spearmint, and her eyes fill up with tears. Her skin is darker, and she's rounder, shorter than I expected. A lot shorter than me. I stand almost even with my dad, which feels right. Like I belong with this group of people.

I'm surprised to find tears welling in my own eyes. I haven't cried in a while, but it feels good to be with them. All at once, I feel wanted.

"It's really you," she says, wonder in her voice. She throws herself at me, sobs into my neck, and I close my eyes and hold her and let out a breath.

"Mama," I whisper into her soft hair. I am at once sixteen, my actual age, and seven, the age they remember me. We are long-lost souls, a mother reuniting with her semi-prodigal son. It is the end of one story and the beginning of the next.

Being near her makes my teeth stop chattering.

# CHAPTER 3

Dad comes in for a group hug, and we are suddenly stepping on each other's feet, not sure where to put our heads in the crowded space. I turn my face outward and see Blake watching. We hold each other's gaze for several seconds, until my eyes cross from staring, and I think, for a moment, that he looks a little bit like this yellow dog I used to see hanging around the group home. He really does. I close my eyes.

The woman from CPS gently interrupts, lays a hand on my coat sleeve. I pull away from my parents. "Ethan," she says, "I'm sorry to intrude. It seems obvious, but I need to ask a few questions." We nod, and she looks at me. "Are these your parents?"

I'm choked up, but I say in a weird voice, "Yes, ma'am."

She asks my parents for identification and they fumble in an attempt to show it as quickly as possible. Asks them officially, "Is this your son?"

Mama breaks down. "Yes," she says, sobbing. "Finally. I can't believe it. Thank you. Thank you so much."

"Please don't be offended by the next question—I'm required to ask. Would you like a DNA test?"

They look at each other and then at me. "Absolutely not," Mama says. "I'm positive."

"There's no need for that," Dad says.

There are a few more questions and papers for them to sign, so we step out of the snow, into the building. At a closed ticket window we spread things out on the ledge, and that's all there is. I already talked to the cops this afternoon. There are no more formalities. It's almost like I got lost in the fishing tackle aisle of Wal-Mart for ten minutes. *This your mom? This your kid? Good. Stay close now, keep a better eye out.*

The woman from CPS squeezes my arm, searches my eyes, and apparently sees what she wants in them—enough to satisfy her that I am okay with all of this. She puts her hand to her chest and says, "Congratulations to all of you." Her voice fills out, like she's choking up. "It's really such an amazing, joyful event when one of the lost ones makes it home again." She smiles brightly, but her eyes glisten. I figure it must feel good to her, like they actually finished a job. To me, it just feels like nausea.

Then the woman turns businesslike. "Mr. and Mrs. De Wilde, we've arranged for our counselor, Dr. Cook, to talk with you all and explain what we know. The train station manager was kind enough to let us use the break room to do this. Ethan, would you like me to stay?" She ushers us to the room and opens the door.

I shake my head. "No, that's okay." It only gets worse the longer she stays. I can't even remember her name, I'm so anxious. Dr. Cook is sitting inside at a round table. I talked to her this afternoon. She has six pencils stuck in the ball of hair at the back of her head—four yellows, two reds.

"All right." The CPS woman steps in after us and introduces my family to Dr. Cook. "Good luck, Ethan," she says. "I'll be in touch in a day or two to see how it's going."

I nod.

Dr. Cook smiles at Blake. "Maybe you and your little sister can sit outside in the waiting area."

Blake glances at Mama and scowls. Mama says, "Yes, good idea."

They go. We sit. And Dr. Cook debriefs.

It's a relief, it really is, to have her talk to my parents instead of me. She tells them everything I told her.

Which, when you think of it, really isn't much at all.

I have three seasons of my life that I want to forget now that I'm here: Ellen (I told them her name was Eleanor—I don't know why), group home, and homeless. My mind wanders and my eyes roam the break room, land on the countertop. Spilled sugar. Coffee stains. A mug with a unicorn on it. For a minute I stare at it, thinking it moved, but it didn't—I'm just tired.

The coffeepot with the orange lid means decaf. I know that from the breakfast place Ellen worked at once in a while, whenever she needed the money. The little bit of coffee left in the pot is starting to burn and I can't look at it. The smell is sharp in my nose. The doctor says, "About two years ago, Eleanor abandoned him in Omaha at a group home." She tells them how I ran away from there and lived at the park and around the zoo. I blow breath out of my nose to get the burned smell out. Finally I just get up and turn off the burner. Dad gives me a curious look, but I don't care. I just don't think having this place burn down right now would make things easier.

Dr. Cook gives Mama the business card of a psychologist who lives near us. Says we should go individually and as a family. All these details are making me twitchy.

When Dr. Cook leaves, we walk out of the break room and find Gracie hopping around the waiting area, babbling about kindergarten, and Blake sitting on the floor against the wall, staring at the ceiling.

"Well, it's official," Mama says with a huge smile, and hugs me again. When she finally lets go, Dad is next. Slaps me hard on the back, right near where my shoulder hurts. I hide a wince and take it like a man.

Blake stands up but doesn't hug me. He stays back, shuffles his feet, embarrassed by absolutely everything. And the girl, the replacement child, she just stares at me.

It's both jubilant and awkward, the five of us all wondering and staring and trying not to get caught looking. Mama apologizes for not bringing balloons. There wasn't time to do anything, she says, and I believe her, since I just called CPS once I made it into Minnesota this morning. They really high-tailed it down here, actually. Must have. And I'm glad for that. I'm grateful. I look around the station, noticing other people for the first time, all of them busy trying to get home, I bet.

We have celebratory hot chocolate from an ancient, faded machine, waiting for the train that will take us home together, a complete family. Dad excuses himself after a minute and I watch him at the ticket counter, buying one more ticket home. My ticket. And I wonder, have they done this before? They didn't want to waste the money in case I wasn't me?

Everyone tries a little too hard. The small talk is strained. Gracie, who's six according to the family website, judges me from a safe distance behind Mama, who is talking excitedly on the phone. Talking about me. I take a sip of my hot chocolate too soon, and now my tongue feels like burlap.

Blake stares at my feet. He was there when it happened—the only witness. Just two brothers drawing with chalk on the sidewalk in front of the house, innocent as can be. I wonder if he remembers it. He doesn't say much. He just glances at me once in a while when he thinks I'm not looking.

"I can't believe it," Mama says over and over to me between calls. "You're all grown up. Such a little boy, and now you're all grown up."

Dad's quiet. He wipes his face with a white handkerchief that he keeps balled up in his hand.

A few times I try to ask a question, but I always change my mind right before I say anything. The words don't sound right. What am I supposed to say? *So, is it always this cold in Minnesota?* Or, *Hey, what have you guys been doing for the past nine years? I see you got busy replacing me.*

On the train it's even harder. We sit in two rows that face each other. I'm by the window, next to Blake. Mama and Dad sit across from us, with Gracie between them. I hold my beat-up old bag on my lap to keep it safe from the slush on the floor. It's so difficult for me to look them in the eyes, like if I do I'm committing to something, even though I'm dying to take in their faces. To get a better picture. They are all looking at me, paying attention to me, asking me simple questions, and actually, I like that. I do. It makes me feel like something.

When there's a lull, I rack my brains for something to say, and I remember the photos on the website. "Still the same old house?" I feel myself starting to sweat again.

Dad clears his throat. "Still the same, yep. Thirty-fifth and Maple." He pauses. "Do you remember it?" His voice is gentle, careful.

"Some of it," I say, careful too. I know it only from the pictures on the website, but I don't want to hurt his feelings. "The front steps and the sidewalk and the white cement driveway, with the grass growing in the cracks. The Christmas tree in the big picture window, and a little black dog—what was his name?" I screw up my eyes, pretending to try to remember, but I already know that I don't know the dog's name. I see the photo of him in my head, but there are so many questions.

"Rags," Mama says with a smile. "Rags died a couple years after . . . about six years ago. Right around when Gracie was born."

"I'm sorry," I say. "He was a nice dog."

Dad laughs. "You hated that dog. He always chewed on your shoes."

"Really?" I laugh too, a little too hard. "I don't remember that."

A few weeks ago, at the library, I found the page—my face staring back at me. My page, with my real name—Ethan Manuel De Wilde—on the National Center for Missing & Exploited Children's website. I Googled my name and saw all the hits. People had been looking for me. Unreal. And then I found my family's website. Even Grandpa and Grandma De Wilde and all the cousins and aunts and uncles post things there. Tons of pictures. Discussions about them . . . and about me. How they've been searching, and how they remember. Memories shared.

Things flash by the window and in my head: sleeping in doorways, the group home in Nebraska, and how I got there . . . and Ellen. . . . My throat hurts. I stare outside into the darkness, watching glowing snow and bare black trees whiz by.

"Um, so, what else do you remember, Ethan?" Blake asks after a while, still not quite looking at me. His voice is nonchalant, but I know what he's really asking. He's asking, *Do you remember me?*

# CHAPTER 4

Instead, I ask him. "Do you remember me? You were just a little kid."

His smile is wary, as if he's still unsure of me. "Sure. You hogged the bed. I kicked you all the time under the covers, and Dad would always blame you because you were older." Blake laughs a little and his voice cracks—he must be going through the horrible voice-change thing.

I smile. "I remember that," I say, even though I don't. Stupid nerves. "I wanted my own bed so bad." I don't know what I'm saying.

Now I just want *a* bed. I don't care if there are seventeen people in it. I need a soft place to rest. My body aches. I've been walking and hitching rides for days. I'd lie on a pile of garbage right about now if it was soft.

I look at Gracie. I'd noticed in my peripheral vision that she was staring at me with her big cow eyes, but now, when I look directly at her, she drops her gaze. *Do you know why they had you?* I want to ask. But I'm not cruel like that. I just stare at her instead, until she hides her face behind Dad's arm.

What else can I say? I'm grateful for Mama, who chatters about the grandparents. Mama's father, Papa Quintero, died about a year ago, which I knew from reading the family message board. I try to feel sad, but he's so distant from me. Besides, he lived in Mexico.

After a while, we are all quiet. Gracie sleeps. Mama says our train ride is about two hours long, and it was already after nine when we left the Red Wing station. I pretend to doze off so I can wrap my head around all of this. All of this newness. Coming back to a family I don't really remember. A pang of . . . of homesickness, I guess, hits me in the gut, and I realize just how badly I want those memories back.

In Belleville we disembark and walk through the parking lot. Blake drops in step next to me, his eyes level with my chin. "You look a little different to me, kid," I say. "I mean, obviously you're a lot bigger. Your hair is darker than it was."

"It always bleaches blond in the summer," Blake says, more talkative under the cover of darkness. "You disappeared in the summer. That's how you'd probably remember me, right? We were outside playing on the sidewalk. Drawing with chalk. I remember it," he says, looking up at me. His eyes narrow a fraction. "I remember the car."

I look sharply at my brother. "You do?" I whisper, but we are at the minivan now, and our conversation ends. I really want to know what my family did in those moments and days after it happened.

We drive home. Home to the white house with black shutters and a big picture window on the corner of Thirty-fifth and Maple. When Dad turns onto Thirty-fifth and slows the minivan, the house looks just like it does in the pictures on the website, only now it's softly lit by the glowing reflection of the moon on snowy ground.

In the front yard stands a weathered family of snowmen:

A man

A woman

A boy

And a girl.

It's them, the four of them.

I am not represented by snow.

Stupid hot tears attack the corners of my eyes, and I feel so unstable. I know it's unreasonable, but I wonder, why didn't they build one for me before they picked me up? Why didn't they just smash them all down so I wouldn't have to see them going on with life without me? As if I didn't matter. As if I didn't exist.

I burst out of the vehicle, breathe in the cold night air to stop the crazy laughter from boiling up, and suppress the urge to run.

# CHAPTER 5

Dad ushers me in first. A fat, orange blob of a cat darts around the corner when I open the door. Inside the house it smells like stew. "Does it look familiar?" he asks anxiously.

"Yeah, a little," I say. But I don't remember any of it. Not this mudroom, not the smells. I thought I'd remember the smells. I try harder, and then I think, yes, somewhere deep down in my brain, suppressed, there it is. That carpety, freshenery, stewy, tiny-bit-of-musty house smell. I assign it a name—home. That's it. That's Home. Everybody starts taking off their boots and hanging their coats on hooks like we do this every day together. But there are only four hooks.

"Oh, goodness," Mama says, realizing it. "I'm sorry.

I'll get another hook up tomorrow." She reaches out her hand.

I stand there, unsure I want to let go of my coat, sock-footed on hard little balls of snow, feeling the cold wetness seep through. "You can use my hook," Gracie says, her shyness having dissipated into the walls of familiarity. She ceremoniously drops her coat and hat on the floor and grins all naughty-like. Like she knows she is in control of this family because of her unique position. I let go and Mama takes my coat from me and hangs it up, and then hangs Gracie's coat over hers.

Two steps lead up from the mudroom to a door to the main part of the house. We walk in, everyone crowding behind me. "You guys go first," I say. I let Blake, Gracie, and Mama scoot past me, and I follow them. I don't need the pressure of them watching me right now, I really don't. I feel like I'm going to crack. Like my head is made of stone.

The kitchen has a few dirty dishes piled up in the sink, and there are bowls with food in them still sitting on the table. But the rest of the house is so clean.

"We left in a hurry," Mama says, apologizing. "It's a bit of a mess, but when we got the call that you were down in Red Wing, well." She sweeps her hand around the room. "You can imagine. Do you want some food? Are you hungry?"

I shake my head. "The lady got me some dinner."

Mama turns to my brother. "Blake," she says in a firm, quiet voice, "can you clear this up, please?" She turns back and beams at me, and then looks upward. "Dear God," she says reverently, clasping her hands together, staring at the light fixture, and shaking her head in wonder, "is it really our Ethan? After all these years . . ." She comes over to me and hugs me again tightly, and then she shoos Gracie to her room to get her pajamas on.

When we hear Gracie's door click shut, Mama gives Dad a meaningful look. Dad nods and beckons for me to follow him and Mama into the living room, so I do.

"Gracie doesn't really know what's going on," he says in a low voice. "She's a little too young for us to explain what happened to you. You understand?"

I feel something twist in my gut. "Yeah, sure," I say. My voice sounds thin in my ears.

"She knows you're her brother and that you are the boy whose picture is on the wall," Mama hastens to add. "We just didn't tell her any details about the abduction. She's only six. We're going to try and make your return as normal as possible for her—for all of us—and send her to school tomorrow as usual. Blake, too. Give you a chance to settle in before the weekend."

"It's okay," I say. I know it's not Gracie's fault. Still, I feel upset about it. "So, if she asks me about things, what do you want me to do, just sort of lie?" I laugh nervously and it comes out like a hiccup. It's a bad habit of mine, laughing at weird times. Somebody could up and punch me in the stomach or say something really horrible to me and chances are I'll just start laughing hysterically, even if it hurts like hell.

"Maybe just be vague," Dad says. He scratches his five o'clock shadow. "I'll bet you were surprised to see her," he says.

"Yeah, a little," I lie. I knew all about her. The website has more pictures of her than anybody else. I just feel bad. I do. I feel bad for having had to relearn everything about them from our little family website—all those years I missed. And I feel bad that I don't remember them—like I didn't care enough or something, you know? There's so much stuff to know. I've been gone for more than half my life.

"There's a lot of things different, I'm sure." Dad smiles. "We'll have time to catch up. We have the rest of our lives now," he says, a little overdramatically. It feels like we're in a movie. He puts his hand on my shoulder and it sits there like it's a parrot, and I'm a pirate, yarrr. I shake my head, trying to concentrate. So tired.

Dad gives me a tour of the house to help me get reacquainted. In every room he asks, "Do you remember this?"

Remember this? Remember that? They want me to remember so badly. Sometimes I say yes, sometimes no. Mostly no, because the yeses give him so much hope. It's hard to watch. Can't stand the pressure of that much hope.

I'm grateful when we return to the living room and Mama has photographs to look at. Me at Christmas in my red footie pajamas. Me at my sixth birthday party, surrounded by children I don't recognize. On Halloween, dressed as Superman. At a lake, wearing a blue swimsuit. I stare at my overexposed face as Mama reminisces.

Blake passes by the entry to the living room, where we sit. He pauses, and then instead of coming in, he walks down the hallway, and I see my chance to talk to him. "Is it okay if I go?" I ask, and I slide out from under my dad's arm and follow Blake, not waiting for an answer. Not looking back.

"Hey . . . ," I call out, trying to catch up with him. I pretend that Dad hasn't just shown me the room, so that I have something to talk about. "So, uh, is our room the same as before?"

Blake snorts. "No. Choo-choo trains? I got rid of that wallpaper a long time ago." He turns into our room and I follow. "I'm not sure what's going to happen now," he says, and I don't know what he means, until I realize he's talking about the furniture.

There's his twin bed, a dresser, a desk, and a chair. It's a small, messy room with clothes piled on the floor. The walls are simple, painted blue. The orange cat I saw earlier has made its way in here and is curled up on the foot of Blake's bed. Blake starts to pick up some of his crap, and I wander to the dresser, which is topped with a variety of books, papers, and mutilated action figures in inappropriate poses. I stare at a framed picture that is semi-hidden behind the clutter. It's a photograph of two boys sitting behind a lemonade stand. I think it's him and me. "Is this us?" I ask.

Blake looks at me curiously. "You don't remember that?"

"No," I say.

"Yes, Ethan. It's us." Blake frowns.

"I figured," I say. Embarrassed. Feeling like I should apologize for my memory. This is going to be awkward, all of this "getting to know each other" stuff.

I'm quiet and Blake is still looking at me, working his jaw. He moves to the door and closes it, and I start to get a weird feeling.

"I remember," he says, his voice low. "The car. You went right to it."

I just look at him. My eyes get wide and I can't stop them.

"Why did you do that?" His voice is strained.

I don't know what to say. I see him winding up, his lips twitching, and I am not ready for this.

"You went right up to those strangers and you got into their car." Blake's face twists and turns red. "You were seven years old, a second grader. You should have known better! You should have known not to go up to strangers. What the heck was wrong with you?" Blake sniffs wildly and presses his fingertips into the corners of his eyes to stop the drips.

"I . . . ," I say. But instead of answering, I go to the door, open it, and slip out, closing it behind me, and I walk slowly past the bathroom, past Gracie's bedroom, down the hall, and through the dining room, to the living room, where Mama and Dad sit, talking quietly. Dad has his laptop out and he's typing. They look up and stop talking when I come into the room.

"We're emailing some more relatives and friends now, but we'll wait until morning to call the rest and let them know you're back," Dad says. "It's late." He goes back to his typing and adds, "Give you a good night's rest and some time to settle in. Then we'll have everybody over to see you tomorrow night. All right?" He looks up and smiles, and it's such a warm smile.

"Yeah, okay," I say. More people.

Mama pats the sofa cushion next to her, so I sit down. "We'll have Blake sleep out here tonight, at least until we can get another bed for his room—your room, I mean, the both of you."

"No, Mama, really," I say. I remember crying out for my mother, vaguely, a long time ago. She loves being called Mama, I know it from one of her stories on the website, so I do it, even though it sounds a little babyish for a sixteen-year-old. "I don't want Blake to sleep out here. I'll sleep here. Trust me, the sofa is about a million times better than where I slept last night."

"Are you sure?" she asks, uncertain.

"Yes, I mean it."

She sighs deeply. "I can't believe it's really you," she says. "It's amazing. . . . We thought we'd found you so many times over the years, but the leads were all dead ends." She shuffles through the pictures of me, putting them into a neat pile on the end table. She looks at me and hesitates. "Do you feel like talking more about that? About how you got home?" Her skin looks so anxious, all crinkled up by her eyes.

"Not really," I say, sorry. "Not right now. I'm so tired."

She pats my hand. "It's okay. We have lots of time to talk."

Later, after midnight, when all the lights are out and I'm lying on my makeshift couch bed, exhausted, I can't sleep. It's too quiet, too . . . too nice. I stare through the moonlight at the framed school portraits on the living room wall. Blake looks like the oldest kid in the family. The Replacement Kid is angelic and perfect. And I am toothless and dumb-haired, perpetually stuck in second grade.

# CHAPTER 6

During the night the phone rings. Twice, three times. I hear somebody scuffling around, but I'm gone from the world.

In the morning I wake up to strange noises and smells, and for a minute I don't remember where I am. I crack open an eyelid and there, staring at me, just standing in the living room all dressed in a freaking snowmobile suit and snow boots and carrying a Dora the Explorer lunch box, is Gracie. She looks like an elf.

"I'm going to school now," she says. She doesn't move.

"So what," I mutter. I remember the other kids in the group home. Sixteen of us, all ages. The head dude had a bratty daughter about the same age as Gracie who always came to the home for lunch after morning kindergarten.

Kimberlee. Couldn't stand her. But there was an abandoned kid who wasn't bad—really shy. I liked getting him to laugh. You never know with little kids.

I struggle to lift my head. My body is stiff. Everything hurts, but it's good, sort of, like the worst ache you feel right before the healing begins. My throat is sore, though, which is making me cranky, and my voice comes out hoarse. "What's in your lunch box?"

Gracie narrows her eyes. "Nofing."

"Seriously?" I laugh a little and then erupt in a short coughing fit. "Come on," I say. "Tell me. I'm not going to steal it."

She stares at me a minute more, all round cheeks and pouty baby lips, surrounded by a mop of brown curls that bounce when she shakes her head.

I try again. "Do you go to all-day school? So that's your lunch?"

"No. I go to kindergarten. It's half-a-days."

"Hmm, I see," I say, still pretending to figure out what's in the box, but I'm getting tired of the game now.

"Mama said to wake you up and tell you to take a shower. She put some clean clothes in the bathroom for you. Grandpa and Grandma De Wilde are coming later. And the newspaper people are here." Only she says it like *noose* paper, and I picture an animated rolled-up paper with those moving black eyes and eyebrows, a big old rope around its neck, or whatever, hanging from a tree and choking to death.

"Noose paper," I say softly, trying out the local accent. "Wait, what? You mean reporters, or the delivery guy?"

Gracie just stares at me. Shrugs.

"Okay, uh . . . where's the washer and dryer?"

"Down the basement," she says, and puts a hand on her hip, too big for her britches.

"And . . . what's that cat's name?"

"Russell."

"Rustle? Like what leaves do?"

"What? No. Like . . . Russ-*oll.*"

"Oh. Is Russ-oll in your lunch box?"

Gracie scowls. "You're dumb. Any more questions?"

"Besides 'what *is* in your lunch box?' No, I don't think so."

"It's my private property, Efan."

I laugh. Precocious little lisping brat. "Okay, well, have a good day at school, then."

She turns to go. "Mama says you're going to school Monday. She has to unroll you first today."

"Oh," I say, and her cuteness is lost on me for the moment.

School.

# CHAPTER 7

I roll over on the couch and watch the morning activities from my dimly lit corner of the living room.

Mama rushes around the kitchen, drying her hands on a towel and grabbing her coat and purse. "Come on, Gracie," she says, and they go out through the mudroom. "I'll be back in a bit, Ethan. Blake's still here and Dad's in the shower. Don't answer the door for any reason, okay? Reporters are starting to show up. . . . I should have known word would leak . . . but don't worry. Back soon." The door slams shut.

Blake, his hair wet, rounds the corner from the hallway and glances at me, and then heads for the kitchen. Stares out the window for a minute, then grabs waffles from a box in the freezer and puts them in the toaster.

"You want some waffles?" he says. A peace offering, maybe.

I sit up on the couch and unwind my legs from the sleeping bag. It's nice to wake up warm. My stomach growls. "Yeah, sure," I say, and shove my legs into my tattered jeans, walk over to the kitchen in my bare feet and stare out the window at the two vehicles along the road. Blake pushes the box toward me. I look at it. Look at him. We wait in uncomfortable silence for his waffles to pop up.

"Look," I say finally, feeling like our conversation from last night needs to be finished. "I don't know why I went with them. I don't really remember anything about any of it, or my life before, you know? She messed with my head. A lot."

Blake shifts on his feet and doesn't acknowledge me. It's quiet again.

The toaster pops up and we both jump. He puts the waffles on a plate and pours syrup on them.

I put mine in and press the lever. "So, I'm sorry," I say. "If I just went with them, if that's what happened . . . I'm really sorry."

Blake swallows hard. I can see his little baby Adam's apple move in his neck. He goes to the table. "Yeah, I know," he says quietly. "I mean, it totally wrecked everything here."

"What was it like?" I try to sound simply interested,

but my legs are shaking from the anxiety—as much as Mama wants to know where I've been, I want to know what happened here, after. I control my face so he doesn't see how badly I want it.

"A disaster." Blake takes a bite. He chews, and then shoves the plate away and stands. Scowls, like he's trying to decide something, and then looks at the clock. "I gotta get to the bus stop." He wipes his mouth on a napkin. "Dad?" he calls out. "Am I just supposed to ignore the reporters, or what?"

I turn away, groaning inside. Wipe my hand over my face, trying to smooth the stress away. I just want to know. Is that so much?

Dad doesn't answer, so Blake walks down the hallway to the bathroom and bedroom. I hear them talking, and then Blake returns with his backpack. He nods when he passes me, like he's the older brother and I'm the younger one. Like he knows I want information and he's punishing me.

I know I'm paranoid. I am. "Don't talk to them," I say. Another TV news truck pulls up.

"Whatever," Blake says. I hear the door to the mudroom opening, the sound of boots, the outer door creaking and slamming shut. From the little window over the sink I see reporters get out of their vehicles and rush toward the house, and Blake heading for the bus stop. He moves faster.

Dad flies through the kitchen to the mudroom, hair still wet and buttoning his shirt. He gets into his coat and boots and I see him jogging through the Minnesota snow, talking to the reporters, protecting Blake. One of the reporters is trying to talk to some of the kids at the bus stop, but he moves back to our driveway when Dad comes out.

Blake makes it to the four-way stop right out front, where the small group of what looks like middle and high school kids stand, waiting for the bus. He walks up to a couple of shorter guys and I watch them all goof around, stealing glances at the reporters. There are girls there too. One of the taller girls, with a red coat, her black hair shooting down her back, stares at Blake, and then looks sharply at our house, into the window, almost like she's looking straight through me. But then she looks away when the bus pulls up. I take a bite of my waffle and wonder if I should know any of them. If I ever played with them. I feel so empty, so . . . nothing. I wonder if Blake will tell them about me.

When I see Mama's car coming around the corner, I rinse my plate in the sink and then go to take my shower. Thinking and thinking about how much more strained all of this is than I expected.

It's been such a long time. The big hunks of life aren't going to come back just like that, no matter how much I want them to.

# CHAPTER 8

After my shower, I slip past Mama on the phone and head to the basement wearing a pair of my dad's sweatpants, safety-pinned to keep them up, and a flannel button-down shirt. Upstairs, the phone doesn't stop ringing. Mama is blabbering excitedly about me, one call to the next. On one call I hear her talking kind of soft to Dr. Somebody, repeating, "Okay, so we'll take it slow, let him talk when he's ready," which is a relief. But then on the next call, she schedules an appointment for me, which is not cool. I think it might be that shrink that Dr. Cook told us about.

The basement is as big as the main floor. There's a finished rec room, bathroom, and laundry area, but half of this level is unfinished. On the far wall is a slider door that opens onto the backyard, and tons of boxes are stacked all around in the unfinished part and also in the rec room.

I dump all of my dirty laundry out of my backpack and into the washing machine—two shirts, two pairs of boxers, two T-shirts, two pairs of ripped jeans, and three pairs of holey socks. And then I throw in my grungy coat, gloves, hat, even my filthy, stinking tennis shoes, and just wander around the basement looking at things while the machine clunks and spins.

There's a pool table down here, and the balls are all over the place, like somebody didn't know or didn't care. I look at all the old toys that are semi–packed away but still accessible. In the corner of the rec room there's a faded orange electric racetrack with two cars, red and blue. I pick up the blue one, turn it in my hand, and stare at it hard, thinking, and something clicks. *This one was mine.*

I set it down on the track and push the button on the controller, but nothing happens. The batteries must be dead.

I look through old, musty-smelling picture books. *Where's Waldo?* and *I Spy*. They're all about finding something, or someone, hidden. I wonder if my family ever played Where's Ethan?

There are tons of memories down here. Against the wall by the pool table, I find boxes with my name on them. I sit down on the floor and open one up. There are toys, pictures, memories of all sorts inside. A collection of rocks and some baseball cards. I pick up each item and inspect it carefully. Some of the pictures are familiar, and I know I've seen them before on the website. I stare at them, stare at little me. I take after Mama, I guess. Blake is fairer, like Dad, and Gracie is darker-skinned with wavy hair like Mama. And like me.

While I'm packing up the boxes again, Mama comes downstairs. "Hey, Ethan," she says. Her voice is so timid. "You doing okay? I'm sorry I've been on the phone so much."

I smile at her. "I'm just . . . yeah. Doing my laundry. Thanks," I say, and then I realize how stupid it sounds to thank my mother for letting me use the washing machine. "So are we going to talk to the reporters?"

"Dad is trying to handle them, but they really want to talk to you. What do you think?" Mama comes and sits next to me on the floor. "It's weird, isn't it?"

"Yeah." I move over so we're not too close. She doesn't seem to notice.

"It's going to be weird for a while."

I picture myself on TV. "Why are they even here?" I know why, but I want to hear more.

"Word got out faster than I expected. I should have known. You're kind of a big deal in Belleville, you know. Massive search, everybody in the community looking for you for weeks." She shifts and peers at me. "Local TV news is asking for an interview here in the house. I said I would talk to you and see how you felt about it. The news crews aren't going anywhere, at least for the time being."

I take it in. "Wow," I say. They really searched for me. I feel so guilty . . . so good, and so guilty. Then, "Yeah. The people should know about my return." I'm so delighted to know they searched that I don't know what I'm saying. *The people should know about my return? Who am I, Jesus Christ?*

"I'll call CPS and have them send someone to be here with you."

I consider it for a minute. "No. I'd rather not."

"Oh," Mama says, surprised. "Are you sure?" Her eyes worry.

"I don't even know any of them. They would just make me nervous."

"Hmm," she says, and then she nods. "Okay, I get that. No CPS."

I give her a grateful smile.

"Do you want me to help you prepare for the questions?" She sounds hopeful.

I'm getting to where I want to be, sort of. But it doesn't feel right. "No," I say. "I don't want to mess it up. I want to sound authentic." My stomach flutters at the thought of the interview. My mind races, thinking about what I'll say, how I'll say it. But then this weird calmness rushes over my skin. I take a deep breath and let it out. It feels right.

I hope the major networks pick it up. I hope *she* is watching. Wherever she is.

I'm dressed by eleven. I hear Dad talking, leading them all inside. They set up in the living room while I am in the bathroom, fingering my hair to look halfway decent but not too neat.

I meet the makeup person in the kitchen and he puts some stuff on my cheeks and lips. It feels gross. And then I go to the living room and sit down on the couch, next to the TV newsperson. She says her name is Alexandra Richards. It sounds like a fake name to me, but I don't mention that.

Alexandra tells me not to look at the cameras, but to act natural and look mostly at her, like we are having a private conversation. She explains what kinds of questions she's going to ask, and I nod, listening. They are all the things I expected—it's just like anybody on TV. And I am ready, I think. So far so good.

Mama comes and sits down next to me, wearing a nice dress, and then Dad comes, straightening his tie nervously. She and Dad will sit there with me and do a segment, too.

But now it's my time. I'm about to be famous, and I think I want that. I do. I get a chill and pinch my fingers together in my lap. Close my eyes when they turn the lights on me and recall everything I've rehearsed in my head. I want to tell the story, but I can't get too detailed. I just can't go there. I open my eyes and take a deep breath, and then we're rolling. Mama puts her hand on my back for support, and I'm glad I have to focus on Alexandra so I don't have to see my parents' faces.

Alexandra to the camera: If you haven't heard the breaking news in Belleville today, you don't know what you're missing—or what's been found. I'm here in the home of Paul and Maria De Wilde, whose son Ethan, as many of you will remember, was abducted nine years ago from the sidewalk right in front of their house. There was a tremendous search effort, but Ethan disappeared without a trace. Today, however, we have a new story. Ethan De Wilde is alive and well and sitting here with me in his own home once again. Ethan, I'm thrilled to be among the first to welcome you home.

Me: Thanks.

Alexandra: Is it good to be back with your family?

Me: Yeah, it's great. A little overwhelming. I just got here last night.

Alexandra: Ethan, it's our understanding here at KNTV News that you were abducted. Your little brother, Blake, who was only four at the time, told your parents that you got into a car with two strangers. Is that true? Is that what happened to you?

Me: That's what they tell me.

Alexandra: What do you mean? Don't you remember?

Me: No, I actually don't. I don't remember much of anything about my life before the abduction.

Alexandra: So you were brainwashed by your abductors? Where were you all this time?

Me: I'm . . . not really sure. For a long time I was somewhere warmer than this. Not as much snow. She—I mean, I ended up in a youth home in Omaha a couple of years ago, and then when things got bad there, I ran away. I was in St. Louis for a while, living at the zoo and in parks and stuff. There was this one librarian guy. He let me hang out at the library and use the computer as long as I didn't disrupt anybody. And I started searching for missing kids. I went through pages and pages of boys who were reported missing over the last twelve years—I wasn't sure how long I'd been living with . . . living with the person who abducted me. And I found me.

Alexandra: What do you mean, you started searching? If you don't really remember your family, how would you know to search?

Me: Once I ended up at the youth home, I started realizing, or remembering or whatever, that I came from somewhere else. It was just cloudy, you know? So I looked on this one website for missing children, to see if anybody reported me missing.

Alexandra: So you're saying that you somehow hung on to that one memory that you came from somewhere else, but you forgot everything else?

Me: Yes . . . that's about right.

Alexandra: Ethan, you seem so poised, so together, so . . . so healthy after all you have been through. I have to ask the question all of Belleville is wondering: Were you harmed? Abused?

Me: Wow, uh . . . ha-ha. You really went there, didn't you. Um . . . jeez. I guess you could say not physically harmed by my abductor, not really. But I don't want to discuss that.

Alexandra: Not physically? What do you mean?

Me: Not . . . not harmed.

Alexandra: Who abducted you, Ethan? Who did this horrible thing to you?

Me: I . . .

# CHAPTER 9

. . . These are the questions I dread, but I thought I could answer them. I thought I could give her up.

I picture her. Ellen. She called me David, until she abandoned me.

She said she loved me. But she never came back.

I look up at Mama. Her face has gone pale in spite of her makeup, and she grips my shoulder now, whispering, "Oh, Ethan . . ." And I feel so cold and twisted up inside. This mother sitting next to me is the one I should love, but I don't. And the mother I do love is the one I should hate. But I can't.

I fall apart.

# CHAPTER 10

Alexandra: Ethan?

Me: I don't know. I don't know.

I feel the mess inside me start to quiver. Mama grabs my hand now, her other arm still around my shoulders, protecting me, and Dad is on the edge of his seat.

Alexandra looks at me for a long moment as I pull away from Mama and sink back into the couch, covering my face. Feeling the panic rise in my gut. Alexandra raises her hand to the camera team. "Cut. Shut it down," she says to them, and they do it. To me, she asks, "Are you okay?"

I shake my head. Embarrassing sobs and inappropriate laughter force their way out like vomit I cannot stop.

I get up and Mama leads me out of the living room, away from the questions, away from the cameras. But I feel exposed in this house.

Mama whispers comfort and encouragement to me, but I tell her I really just need to be alone. She stares at me for a long minute, then nods and squeezes my shoulder and goes back out to do her piece for the news crew. I don't want to listen. Instead, I sneak downstairs in the dark and burrow out a place for me among boxes marked ETHAN and books about lost things.

# CHAPTER 11

Things are happening backward. I didn't want it to be like this, out of control. Emotional. I feel like I really fucked this up.

I lie curled up on my side on thin green carpet in my basement hideout and try to figure out how I can fix this mess. I'll explain to Mama that I felt threatened by the reporter and that's why I was crying. I'm just not ready to talk about Ellen yet. I mean, everybody in my life now—they're all strangers. All of them. You don't just blurt out stuff like that to strangers when you have no ally. I hear their voices and footsteps above my head and, not long after, the steady, soft rumble of the reporter and crew walking from one end of the house to the other. Doors closing.

Mama doesn't come after me and I'm glad. I wonder if she even saw me sneak down here, if she's worried about where I am. I hear her footsteps overhead walking from one part of the house to another, as if she's looking for me. But soon I hear her at the top of the stairs, calling down, "It's time for me to pick up Gracie from kindergarten. Dad's working in the den. He'd love to talk if you want to, just go on in—but we understand if you need some alone time. I left you some lunch up here . . . it's your favorite sandwich." She pauses. "Maybe later you and Gracie and I can go shopping, get you some clothes and toiletries and things of your own before Grandpa and Grandma come over. I'm locking the doors, so don't, you know . . . don't go anywhere. Don't let anybody in." She laughs anxiously, like she knows how paranoid that sounds, but keeps going. "Just stay inside while I'm gone, okay?"

She doesn't wait for me to answer; she just goes. I like that. Maybe she's not too pissed at me for ruining the taping after all.

A while later I go upstairs and sit at the table, where there's a sandwich wrapped in plastic on a plate. I unwrap the sandwich and stare at it, open it up carefully. Bologna and smashed potato chips between two pieces of buttered white bread. "This is my favorite?" I mutter, and then I take a bite. It's not half bad. I get up and grab a soda from the fridge, and then I feel weird, like maybe there's a rule about soda at lunchtime like at the group home, so I put it back and drink water instead.

The phone rings three times while Mama is gone. I don't answer it, but once I hear Dad talking from the den.

Mama and Gracie come home just as I finish eating. "Thanks for the sandwich," I say sheepishly as Mama gets the bread and bologna out again, this time for Gracie.

"Of course! How are you feeling?" When Mama finishes making Gracie's sandwich, Gracie presses it flat with her hand so that the chips crunch.

"Fine." I watch Gracie eating. She's like a flamingo, all pink and poised. "Didn't you already have lunch?" I ask, pointing to her lunch box, picking up the game again.

"Mama," she says coolly, looking straight at me. "Efan is trying to get into my private property."

"Now, Gracie. Be nice. He's just curious," Mama says, phone to her ear and distracted as she's trying to listen to the voice mails.

I flash Gracie a triumphant look.

She scowls and takes her lunch box to her bedroom.

With Gracie gone, Mama comes over to me and hugs me. Holds me tight and whispers, "I'm sorry about the TV thing."

"Me too. It was my fault."

"Not a chance. You're perfect." She doesn't let go. Just

asks, still whispering, "So . . . that woman Eleanor didn't hurt you?" She can hardly get the words out before she's crying again.

"No, Mama," I say. "No. She didn't hurt me. She just wanted a kid." I want to tell her how it really was with Ellen. I want to. But I can't hurt Mama like that, and I need to stop thinking about it now so I can focus on remembering. I just pat her back and let her cry it out.

We go to the mall. Mama asks what styles I like, and I don't know the answer.

"You're supposed to wear your jeans so your butt hangs out," Gracie says when Mama goes off to find more shirts.

I laugh. "Then my butt gets cold. I'm tired of being cold."

"Why did you live outside, then? How come I never seen you before if you're my brother?"

I look at Gracie in one of the mirrors. "I went away. A long time ago, before you were born. I lived somewhere else. And then that person couldn't take care of me anymore so she dropped me off at a bad place. And I ran away and lived on the streets until I found you. I even lived at the zoo for a while."

"Ha-ha, the zoo!" Gracie says. She ponders it for a while. "I would have runned away too."

I nod. "Of course you would have. Because you're smart like me."

She laughs. "I'm smarter than you."

"Oh, really?"

"Yeah."

"How?"

"I wouldn't have gone away from Mama in the first place. Why'd you do that?"

I'm grateful to see Mama coming back with more stuff. "I dunno why, kid," I say to Gracie. "Maybe you can teach me how to be smarter." My sarcasm is lost on her.

When we get home, Dad is in the garage unloading a bed frame and a mattress from the back of the minivan. I help carry them into the house. Everything inside me wants to ask for my bed to be set up downstairs so I can have a place of my own, but I don't dare. I don't want to sound ungrateful. So we set it all in the hallway outside Blake's bedroom until we can move his crap around to make space for mine. It's going to be a tight fit.

I go out to the garage to close the minivan's hatch when the school bus pulls up in front of the house. I slam the door hard, and then turn and watch as a dozen kids get off the bus. Shivering like crazy, I fold my arms across my chest. It's fucking freezing in this state.

Blake is the third one off. And there's the group of

girls. Some of them look at me, all shy and curious, and some are oblivious. The girl in the red coat I saw this morning yells good-bye to her friends and turns in the opposite direction from them, but stops in her tracks when she sees me. She catches up to Blake in the driveway and walks with him. Says something that makes him laugh. She's a little taller than him, and when they approach, I can tell she's older than him. My age, maybe. I'm guessing I'm supposed to know her.

"Hey, Ethan, wow," she says. "I can't believe it's really you." She has crow-black hair and deep, dark eyes, not quite perfect teeth and big, soft-looking lips, the kind you want to bite. She hops in place, apparently excited to see me, which feels nice. Despite the slicing cold wind, I feel a stirring and shove my hands in my pockets.

"Hey," I say, teeth chattering, looking at Blake for help. "Um . . ."

"It's Cami," Blake says, rolling his eyes like I'm stupid. "She's lived down the street since birth?" He says it like a question, as if making me feel stupid will bring her back to my memory.

"I'm sorry," I say, looking back to her, and boy, am I sorry. "I don't remember much."

She grins. "It's okay. I can't believe you're back. Everybody thought you were dead."

"Yeah, I figured." I'm sure I'll hear that a few more times before everybody settles down, too. It's a pretty sick thing to say to somebody, if you ask me.

"I cried for weeks. It was horrible. You were my best friend. We took baths together when we were babies. Our moms used to be friends, back when . . ." She trails off, not embarrassed, but looking at me curiously, like she hopes I remember.

"Wow." I don't know what to say to that. Taking baths together. Jesus. I just look at my feet and stomp them on the garage floor, watching the fluffy new snow skitter away, leaving my footprints looking huge, like a monster's. "I'm sorry I don't remember you. I wish I did."

"You look different," she says then. "Not how I pictured you."

"I need a haircut." I shrug, trying not to blush thinking that she'd been picturing me. But blushing in the cold wind probably wouldn't make a difference anyway.

"When are you coming back to school?"

"Monday, I guess."

"Cool. Well, I gotta get home. See you around?"

"Yeah . . . we're having a party or something tonight, so I'm sure you're invited. . . ."

She grins, reaches out, and squeezes my upper arm, then turns and waves over her shoulder.

I wave back like a dork.

Blake scowls at me.

"What," I say.

"Dude. How could you possibly not remember *her*?"

He shakes his head and we turn to go inside.

# CHAPTER 12

What starts out as a quiet visit by Grandpa and Grandma De Wilde turns into an extended family reunion. And after the six o'clock news hits, the neighbors start coming too. The phone rings nonstop and finally Dad turns the ringer off and lets everything go to voice mail. People bring food and drinks and it gets really loud.

I recognize some people, aunts and uncles and cousins, from the photos I had studied. But after about the millionth time of having people expect me to know who they are, and then the disappointed looks on their faces when I don't, I get kind of sick of it. It's so hard letting people down over and over again. It's making me feel a little out of control, and I get that anxious skittering in my stomach again.

Finally, I escape. I throw on my new winter coat and step out to the side of the house that is blocked from the wind, and I suck in the freezing night air. My cousin—I think his name is Pete or Phil or something—is out here too, having a smoke, so I bum one, wanting it so bad but hating myself for doing it, because I quit like a year ago. But I can't help it. This is all a little too much.

I'm glad when Phil-Pete leaves so I can be alone, clear my head. And here I stand, freezing my balls off, sucking down a cigarette, and wishing for some of the booze that is flowing inside the house, when across the frozen freaking tundra comes a sweet red coat of distraction.

I bury the cigarette in a snowdrift, wishing I hadn't smoked it, but loving the fleeting rush. Wishing I had a mint. Wishing I could remember Cami, even just a little bit. Her looks remind me of a girl I hooked up with at the youth home—Tempest, her name was—only Cami has class. My gut tightens. I step out into the wind.

"Hey, Cami," I call out.

She's walking up the driveway, hovering over a dinner plate, shielding it, and her hair is going wild. "Hey. What are you doing out here?"

"I needed to get away from the noise."

"It's freezing."

I wave off her concern. "Cookies?"

"Brownies. From my mom. We're all really glad you're home."

"Thanks." I remember what she said earlier. "Why aren't our moms friends now?"

A gust of wind nearly upends the plate in Cami's hand. Her teeth chatter. "I don't know, exactly. But I think it's because maybe your mom couldn't handle it once you were gone. My mom still had me, but your mom didn't have you. Constant reminder. That's what my mom thinks."

I nod and try to shield her from the wind. "That would be hard, I suppose."

We go inside.

It always happens like this for me, you know? Blindsided by a girl. Back with Ellen in Oklahoma, when I was thirteen, there was this girl, Bree Ann, in the apartment next door. Her mother left her alone a lot too. She was older, fifteen, maybe. I used to listen for her. Climb out the window to the fire escape when I heard her go out there to smoke or write in her little notebook. I longed to jump across just to be closer. We didn't ever talk, and she ignored me, but she was my secret and I loved her. I did. I loved just being near her. I wanted to get closer, sit down with her. Talk to her. But back then, before I had to really go out and learn how to get what I wanted, I didn't dare.

I guess I just wanted Ellen to come home, but she was always out working her johns . . . or partying, toward the end of things. That was right before she got rid of me. Everybody gets caught up sometime, she said.

I watch Cami talk to my mother and father and I can hear that laugh. It's like a cat bell, so pretty yet alarming, because I know I'm letting myself fall when maybe I should fly away. But that loneliness inside, it's so fucking painful. It's that longing feeling that scratches to escape and makes you want to blurt out all kinds of gushy crap just to get the girl to look at you. It's like I had with Bree Ann, trying to guess her schedule every day so I'd know when I could just be near her, and a little bit with Tempest, who was always disappearing. I hate it. Love its melty-ness and hate its leash around my neck.

When she's done talking to them and I can pry myself away from other guests I don't remember, she says near my ear, "Let's get away from the mob. Go talk somewhere."

I shiver and nod. We find a spot on the basement steps, away from the noise. Close the door to the rest of the house, and sit. I lean against the wall and she hugs her knees.

"What's your favorite color?" she asks.

"Black."

She laughs. "You can't have black as a favorite color."

"Why not? It's all the colors. Maybe I have a hard time committing to just one." I smile. "What's yours?"

She laughs again and says, "Mine's green. Yours used to be red. What do you like to do for fun? Do you ski?"

"I don't know how," I say. "I'm not really accustomed to this perpetual snow thing . . ." I run my fingers over the carpeted step between us. Brushing it one way, then the other, seeing the color change slightly.

"Skateboard? How about music?"

I look up at her. "Nope, never tried it. Music is nice, I guess."

"Rock, emo, screamo, ska? Punk? Pop? Not country, I hope." She looks at me expectantly.

I feel like I know what I'm supposed to like, but I really don't know that much about music, especially current stuff—just that canned music they play on downtown streets and at the zoo. I shrug. "I like all kinds. Not country."

"Me too."

"Cool," I say. My tongue is in a knot. I'm so surprised she's not asking me all the usual questions I've been bombarded with all night. All the tough questions. Like where the hell was I for the past nine years and what did the evil abductor do to me? Like how was it living in a youth home and on the streets?

"Did you go to school at all while you were away?"

She pulls her hair in front of her shoulder and smiles at me. So easy.

I just look at her a minute, contemplating the question, and I feel myself smiling back—I can't even help it. "Yeah," I say. She makes it comfortable. "At first, I don't think I did—I can't remember. But then yes, some of the time. We moved around a lot, so I was always catching up."

"I'm really glad you're home," she says. "And it's cool to see inside your house again. It's been a long time."

"You haven't been over? I thought you were sort of friends with Blake."

She laughs. "Nah. We just ride the bus together. He's just a kid, you know? I think he has a little crush on me, actually."

The crowd noise increases suddenly and Russell shoots down the stairs like a gremlin. I look up. Blake stands at the top, glowering. "Mom needs you," he says. He looks from me to Cami, then back to me, and slams the door. I look at Cami and her eyes are wide.

"Gosh," she says. "I hope he didn't hear that."

I shrug. "Don't worry, he probably didn't. I think he's mad at me. Besides, I don't blame him."

"For what?"

I stand up. But I don't want to go. "Having a crush on you."

Cami blushes and stands up too. Climbs the stairs. "I should go," she says. "I'll see you Monday?"

I bite my lip. "Yeah, I guess."

She gives me a hug, and that freaking kills me. It really does.

# CHAPTER 13

Friday night doesn't end until Sunday. The visitors keep coming. Another newspaper and TV crew show up to do a story, and Mama makes them give us the questions first so we can approve them. Somewhere during that time, two uncles and an aunt barge into Blake's bedroom to construct my bed.

By the end of it, when Dad finally closes down the circus and says "enough," Gracie is cranky from too much attention and sweets, Blake is disgusted by being ignored and trampled, Mama is frazzled, and I've got a major headache from all the stress, noise, and stupidity. I escape to the basement for some privacy and hold my ears to stop the ringing sounds.

Later, after lights-out, Blake won't even talk to me.

I wish he would accept me, but I just lie in my new bed and feel like I'm taking up space.

Monday morning I'm wide awake at five, thinking about school. Wondering where they'll put me. My chest is in a vise grip. I can't breathe. I start wheezing, sweating, and I get out of bed so I don't wake up Blake. Walk to the bathroom and just sit in there, on the edge of the bathtub, trying to get a grip. I drape a towel over my head and breath in and out, in and out. In. And out.

In the shower I think about Cami. That helps me calm down.

I'm ready for school two hours early, so I just sit at the dining table drinking about forty-nine cups of coffee. I watch, like I'm a security camera, the people moving through the house and sitting at the table for a few minutes to eat, then going on their way, first Dad, then Mama and Gracie, then Blake. If we talk, I don't remember what we say. Mama gives me some papers and talks to me, a concerned look on her face. "You're enrolled and you're all set. Are you sure you don't want me to go with you? Set you up with the school counselor?"

But I can't comprehend right now. I shove the papers in my backpack. "No, I've had lots of first days at schools. I know the drill."

"Okay," Mama says, doubtful. "Come straight home after and tell me how it went."

I just nod. "I'm good, Mama. I know what to do." I am in a zone, a place I need to be to keep away the panicky things inside me.

Still, it's been a while since I went to school. Like, a really long time.

At the bus stop, Blake stands off to the side, watching me. He calls out to a few guys who are near me. They ignore him. He pretends like he doesn't care, but his face is hard, and I feel bad for him. I can tell he's not a popular kid, and that worries me, because maybe I'm not popular either. I wonder how big the school is. Maybe I'll be just a blip.

Cami is at the bus stop, and she smiles at me but lets the others crowd around me. I talk to them, but I stare at her until she blushes. I want to talk to her more. Have her ask me easy questions that don't stress me out. And I want to know what everyone did, what things were like right after it happened. I want her perspective.

I want her.

She's a fucking lake of beautiful.

On the bus, I shove into the seat with her. The other girls give sidelong glances and carry on stupidly, but I don't care. "Hey," I say.

She looks at me and blinks her ropey lashes. "What are you doing?"

"Why? Is this seat taken?"

"My friends . . . ," she says.

"Tough," I say, but I smile.

She laughs and gives in, shrugging to the other girls and moving her backpack from between us. "You nervous?"

The vise grip tightens on my ribs. "Nah. I'm cool."

"Oh, I see," she says with a lopsided grin. Teasing me. "I thought if you were nervous I could show you around, but . . ."

I slouch in the seat, stick my knee up against the seat-back in front of us, and lean my head back. My heart races from all the caffeine this morning, and from the closeness of this girl. "So, what—you only show the nervous loser-type guys around, not the cool ones who used to be your best friend? What kind of person are you?"

Cami shrugs, takes her wool cap off, and smoothes her hair down. "I help those in need. You, apparently, don't need anything."

Oh, God. I need her.

In school, she walks with me to the office and pauses outside the door. "You'll figure it out," she says. "The layout is just two big squares. Numbers go up, clockwise starting here." Her hair is staticky and I want to touch it. I want her electricity. But she just grins and leaves me there to fend for myself.

I walk up to the desk, where a woman sits with a pen and papers strewn around her, severe black glasses that look kind of artsy, and cropped black hair. A nameplate says her name is Miss Lester.

"Yes?" she says, still writing.

I clear my throat. "I'm . . . Ethan. De Wilde. New student."

The woman looks up. "Oh. Very good. Welcome home. You're that lost boy." It's not a question.

"Yes, ma'am," I say.

She takes my paperwork and shuffles through it, then pulls one sheet out and hands it to me. "You're going to need this—it's your schedule. There's a map on the back. Come with me. We'll put you in classes for now and each teacher will assess you, do some testing, so we know if you're in the right place."

We meet the principal and the school counselor and then she walks me through my schedule. It's easy and I'm really just anxious to get away from her. She walks me back to my first period, and thankfully I get a seat without too much staring.

I don't know anybody in my classes. At lunch, I just sit alone in the middle of the cafeteria and people mostly come and go around me, but some of them say they know me. I tune most of it out and smile when I'm supposed to. Sometimes I pretend to remember something—it's almost a sport now, after the weekend family disaster.

The teachers are decent enough not to make some big announcement about me being there, although one of them, Ms. Gibbons, gets a little gushy, calls me a hero and a survivor. In the hallways, a few people stop me and say stupid "I thought you were dead" things, but I try to stay low-key. I mean, how do you answer that? "Thank you"? Eyes on the ground or on the map, scowl on my face. Most of them either don't remember because they were too young, or they don't really care. Fine by me.

When the bell rings at the end of the day, I manage to find my locker again. I grab my stuff and take off to the bus, stuck behind foot traffic. The crowd shifts and moves as one huge mass. Finally, I bust through the doors to the bus line. My stomach twists when I see her long, black hair.

And the guy who's touching it.

# CHAPTER 14

And then they're kissing. He's leaning back against the bus and she's leaning into him. And I—I'm suddenly doubled up in hysterics, laughing uncontrollably with a crowd all around me, feeling like a total psycho loser and unable to stop it, so I drop down to one knee. Start tying my shoe. Gasping and laugh-crying down at the snow-packed cement as people bang into me, their knees catching my kidneys and shoulders and digging in a little harder than they need to, because I'm there, in their way.

When I finally get it under control, I stand up, take a deep breath and let it out, and move past Cami and the asswipe. I get on the bus and sit up against the window, staring out at them.

I have no idea what to do when she climbs on the bus, alone, and sits with me.

"How was it?" she asks.

"How was what?"

"Your first day, duh."

"Fine." The bus chugs out of the lineup and we're moving, heading toward the middle school, where we pick up the next load of students.

She just looks at me. "Is something wrong?"

I want to yell. Not at her. Just loudly. Scream, so the crap and buildup of everything can get out. I want to hurt somebody. Anybody. Seriously, I could beat the crap out of a little kid right now. I grip my knees and talk myself through it.

The feeling passes.

"Ethan?" She leans in, concerned, and I can smell her. Jesus. Baths together. Fuck.

"I'm fine," I say, and change the subject. Blurting it out. "Tell me what happened after."

"After school?"

"After I disappeared."

She slumps back in the seat. "Oh." She shakes her head. "Oh, that." She takes a deep breath. "It was pretty terrible. Are you sure you want to know?"

"Yes," I say, smiling through gritted teeth. "Please." We come to a stop in front of the middle school just as the students start streaming out of the building. There is chaos as they load. They are so loud. I want them to shut up. Blake raises an eyebrow as he walks past our seat, but says nothing.

"Well, from what I remember, I guess Blake told your mom that you got into a black car. Then your mom called my mom, all hysterical. She asked if you were at our house. Of course you weren't. So we all went out and started looking around the neighborhood for you, and Blake kept yelling about you getting into the backseat of the car. Then the cops came and I guess they got the word out to look for a black four-door, but that's all the information they had."

I am lost in the description. "It was gray inside," I say softly, imagining it, but I have no idea where I get that from. I didn't remember the abduction, but now, it sort of feels like I do, a little. Like hearing the story fills in a little piece of my life.

"The whole neighborhood was looking. We walked for hours, after dark with flashlights, and in shifts for days afterward. Calling out for you. But if you were in a car, I don't know why we spent so much time in the neighborhood. I think maybe people weren't sure they could believe Blake. He was really little."

"Maybe that's why he's so pissed," I say, looking out the window.

Cami shrugs. "I just thought he was so sad about what happened."

I don't know what to say.

"We searched for you for, like, three weeks. It was on the news every day."

We sit in silence. I think about it all. Wonder if they would have found me if they'd just believed Blake.

"Hey, Ethan?" Cami touches my thigh.

"Yeah?" I stare at her hand. I think I can probably take the asswipe, once I get all my strength back and beef up a little. Maybe.

"My mom taped the news. When it happened, I mean. It's on a video. You want to see? I think our VCR in the minivan still works."

I nod and focus. "Yes," I say. "Yes."

We get off the bus and walk to her house. She gets the key from inside and starts up the minivan. "We used to take this beast on trips when I was little. I have an older brother, you know," Cami says. "Josh. He's in college now. We used to fight about what videos to watch." I like how thoughtful she is, letting me know she has a brother without making me feel stupid about not remembering things. We sit in the middle row of the old minivan in her driveway. The engine is running, but the heat hasn't choked its way out yet. Our combined breath fogs the windows, and I'm freezing. Cami leans forward and messes with the VCR, trying to get the tape to play. "I used to watch this over and over," she says simply. "I had a really hard time letting you go."

I think I am in love.

It's a short clip, about four minutes. There are large photos of me, the perpetual toothless second grader, flashing as the anchor talks, with a 1-800 phone number to call. The news anchor looks a little bit fake in his concern over my well-being, but the coanchor looks on like she really cares. There is footage of a group of people tromping through the woods and calling my name—they sound frantic. Then the anchor shows a piece from a news conference on the steps of the police department. My parents huddle together behind a podium, crying, pleading for my return. And there's Blake, four years old and scowling at the sun in his eyes. Mama begs for the abductors to bring me back, no questions asked as long as I'm safe. There's even a reward.

I watch, horrified. Awed. When it ends, I just stare at the screen. After a minute, Cami turns it off and I ask, quietly, "Can I watch it again?"

She peers at me. Pulls off her mitten and touches my cheek. Her finger comes away wet, shiny. "You sure?"

"Yes," I breathe. I want to see it again.

Cami rewinds and I watch it again. All of it. I watch how sad they are, how much they are weeping over me. I drink it in.

"God," I say when it's over. I slump back in the seat and fling my arm over my face, wiping my cheeks and eyes. "God. I had no idea."

"No idea of what?"

I roll my head from side to side on the back of the bench seat, staring at the ceiling of the minivan. "No idea anybody cared like that," I say.

Cami is quiet for a while. And then she says, "A lot of people cared. Tons." She turns sideways toward me on the bench seat, rests her elbow on the back, and just looks at me. "How could we possibly not care?"

I don't want to explain. I already sniveled in front of her. I'm not going to do that again. She probably thinks I'm a freak. "I guess because nobody ever found me," I say. "How would I have known anybody tried?"

"We tried."

"I know that now."

"Good."

And then it's awkward, the two of us alone in a quiet, slowly darkening minivan. Two strangers who used to be friends. But I can feel something here between us. Different from any of the other girls. Deeper. Maybe I'm imagining it. Or maybe this just means something, to have these ties that go back so many years. Maybe you don't have to remember something for it to be true. For it to exist.

She's looking at me, a little afraid about her feelings,

maybe. A little guilty. Probably thinking about the boy-friend. But wanting it—this thing between us. That's probably the best way for her to be, though. Wanting. The wanting always keeps you on your toes, makes you fight for more. I know that well enough.

"I should go," I say. "Homework."

"Yeah, me too." She bites her lip and looks down. I hope she's not looking at my crotch.

I scramble up, suddenly self-conscious, and bump my head. "Shit." I start laughing uncontrollably, but manage to contain it so I don't quite sound like a lunatic. Score.

She laughs and climbs up over the seats to turn off the minivan's engine. Pulls the keys out. "See you tomorrow?"

I shrug, open the slider door, and hop out. She follows. The freezing wind flips my hair off my face. "If I don't get abducted," I say with a grin, but it doesn't really sound funny. "Thanks for showing me the tape. That was . . . that was cool of you."

She stands there, head cocked and tape in hand, like she's trying to decide something. "You want it?" She holds it out to me.

"Nah. I'm good." I've seen enough. More than enough, probably. I turn and grab my backpack and trudge home through the yards, past the snow family that does not include me, and into my house.

# CHAPTER 15

Gracie's stirring mushy chocolate ice cream in a bowl when I walk in the kitchen. Mama looks up sharply. Comes over and hugs me a little too tightly, and then pushes back. "Where were you?" she asks.

I set my backpack down in a chair. "I went over to Cami's after school."

"Oh," Mama says. She presses her lips together and turns her face away. I can see her take a deep breath and let it out.

"Why, what's up?"

"You're sposta call Mama if you're going to be late, even one minute. That's the family rule," Gracie says.

Mama nods, grim-faced. "I didn't tell you, Ethan. I guess I didn't expect you to go anywhere on your first day."

"Blake didn't tell you? He saw me go." I grab Gracie's spoon just as it's going up to her lips and shove the glob of ice cream into my mouth.

"Hey!" she yells, and slams her elbow into my hip. "Mama! Efan stole my ice cream and got his gross germs on my spoon!"

But Mama's distracted. I grin at Gracie, pushing melted ice cream through my teeth. She scowls and takes her bowl with her to get a new spoon, grumbling, and then she moves to the other side of the table.

I swallow it and turn back to Mama, realize she was really worried. "I'm sorry I didn't call. I should have thought of that."

"Yeah, it's sort of a family thing, after what happened." Mama glances at Gracie, and I know that means not to say anything scary.

"I can see why you'd want to know where everybody is," I say. And I *can* see it now. After the tape. "But I don't actually know the phone number here."

"It's on one of the papers I gave you this morning, remember? I told you. I showed it to you." She looks freaked again and her voice is on the fringe of yelling. "You have that sheet, right? Please check."

"Oh, yeah," I say. I'm sure she's right. "Yeah, I have it. Sorry, I just forgot." I watch her cautiously.

She waits for me to check, so I do. Sure enough, there

it is. I feel her eyes boring into me. And for a second, I wonder why I ever left the freedom of the street.

She smiles, finally. "Good. I'm getting you a cell phone tomorrow. Please make sure you always let me know where you are. And can you memorize the home phone number? Please?" She's calmer now.

"Great. Okay. I will," I say. A cell phone? I have exactly no one else to call. It will be like a leash to my mother. Nice. Quite the reality check seeing the overprotective side of her.

And then we just stand there, quiet, awkward, so I start my homework at the table so Mama can hawk all over me.

I want to talk about things. I do. But it's so hard. We can't do it when Gracie's around, and when we're alone, it's so hard to start the conversation. It's like the words weigh a thousand pounds each. So I don't say anything.

At dinner, all five of us sit around the table like a TV family and talk about our days. I have never, ever done this before. With Ellen, it was so laid-back—we ate whenever we had food, wherever we happened to be standing. Once again, I feel like I'm on a TV show. I wonder what each of them is thinking. If it's as weird for them as it is for me.

I help with the dishes afterward, and then go and hide down in the basement for a few hours, making my space more comfortable with an old quilt I find in the bottom drawer of a beat-up dresser. And then I look for more treasures in my Ethan boxes. The building blocks and collectible cards and books, all neatly packed. Shoe boxes filled with school report cards and math papers and art projects Mama saved. And the photos. I stare and stare at myself, trying to absorb that part of my life, those first seven years. But it's all still so cold. Looking at the photos is like looking at pictures of myself superimposed in strange settings. I memorize everything.

It's each of us in our beds, in the dark, when Blake says, "You're hooking up with Cami, I suppose."

I hear jealousy in his voice, but I might be wrong. "No," I say.

"Why not?"

I open my eyes and stare into the darkness. "She's got a boyfriend."

"No she doesn't."

"Yeah, he just doesn't ride the bus."

"Oh." Blake doesn't sound convinced.

Silence.

"So," I say. "You want to tell me what it was like?"

Blake is so quiet, I think he's sleeping. But then, after a while, he says, "I was just really mad at you. That's what I remember. Being mad."

"It's okay." I just want him to say it and get over it, so things aren't so weird.

"Why did you do it? Why did you go with strangers in that car?"

"I don't know, Blakey." I heard Gracie call him that once.

There's another pause. "You used to call me that. You're the one who started that nickname."

"I know," I lie. I just want him to love me.

To forgive me.

He's quiet for a minute. "You have no idea how you wrecked everything. Mama and Dad started fighting all the time. Crying. Nobody gave a crap about me. It was all about you. And then when we finally got a little bit used to you being gone, me all alone with them, Mama not crying ten times every day, there was the baby."

"I'm really sorry."

I hear Blake roll over, turn his back to me, and then he says, muffled, "It's still all about you. Always will be. Both of you. You guys are like . . . I don't know. The Lost Boy and the Miracle Girl who took his place."

# CHAPTER 16

I lie awake in bed for a half hour, thinking, before I climb out and go to the kitchen for a drink. Russell is roaming the house, stalking shadows. I picture him on the street, where we'd be enemies competing for food. Inside, we are friends. I give him a cat treat, take my water with me, and wander to the living room, where I see a soft glow of light.

Mama's still up. She's in her bathrobe in the dark, watching a late show with the sound on low. The only light is from the TV. She motions for me to come.

I sit down next to her on the couch. "Hey."

"Can't sleep?"

"Nope. You?"

Mama smiles. "Same. This is all really crazy, isn't it. You doing okay?"

The TV flashes. "Yeah. Pretty much."

"I set an appointment for you to see a psychologist. The one that CPS recommended to me is on vacation this week, so we're in for next week. Okay?"

I bite the inside of my cheek and say the right thing. "Yeah. I suppose."

"I know it's got to feel really strange to be here. We're all so glad you're back, Ethan. We really are. It's just going to take some adjusting for all of us."

Adjusting. It's pretty much all I do—I am an expert. "I've made adjustments before."

"Have you? Like what?"

And there it is. An opening. I feel her lean toward me just a fraction. Eager, but not pushing me.

I take a breath and let it out. Deciding. "The woman who . . . had me. Um . . . Eleanor." I'm not sure why I want to keep protecting Ellen's name, but I do. "After a while, after everything—having me for all those years—she got rid of me. Couldn't afford to keep me anymore. She drove me out to Nebraska to a youth home. You can drop your kids off there in Nebraska, did you know that? No penalty. Leave 'em for good," I say. "And people do it. She did that."

Mama wears an intense look. She's quiet, but I can tell she's disturbed, and I like that, actually. Is that sick?

"So," she says. "You had to adjust from Eleanor's home

to the group home." Her words are clippy and her accent gets sharper. I can tell that she has a thousand other questions, but she holds them in.

"Yes."

"That must have been hard."

I remember it. Remember Ellen pulling up to the door in the darkness, leaning over me to read the letters on the glass. Telling me to go on, it was okay, that she'd be back for me in a few days, once she got a job and could get us a new place in Omaha. Touching my cheek, telling me she loved me, and I could see in her eyes that she meant it. I believed her. I did.

And then I had to live it down. All the other abandoned loser kids mocking me. Up in my face. They knew. Even my girl Tempest said Ellen wouldn't be back. But I was stupid. It was months before I believed them. Before I believed that Ellen could ever do anything so horrible to me. When I fell apart, they all fucked with my head even more.

"It was hard," I agree.

"Then what happened?" She asks. Her voice is soft, like she's scared I'll run away if she asks it too loud.

"I stayed awhile longer and got beat up a few times. Learned how to fight back. But that's where I started thinking that maybe, you know, maybe there was a family, a long time ago. Before Eleanor. Finally I ran away and lived on the streets for about a year before I found you."

Mama squeezes my knee, and then she hugs me. "I'm glad you found us. We tried so hard to find you. We really did."

"I know." I hug her too. Something thaws inside me. It's starting to feel real, being here.

Mama hangs on, clutching the back of my shirt. I can hear her crying a little on my shoulder, and then she starts sobbing. I pat her back. It's awkward and I hope it stops soon. I can't take this every day. But she's a nice lady, and she's my mama no matter what I remember about her, so I let it happen.

"I'm so sorry," she says, sniffling. "I'm so sorry I didn't watch you better. I wish I could have that minute back. Over and over I wish it. I can't forgive myself."

"Mama, it's okay," I say.

And for a moment, it is.

# CHAPTER 17

At breakfast Dad looks at me with a half smile that says Mama told him everything. I'm glad not to have to repeat it. I down some coffee and grab my backpack, trying to decide what my Cami approach will be today. I think I'm going to pretend I'm not interested.

Blake and I head out to the bus stop and it's so cold my nose hairs freeze. Cami's there already, hovering near the other girls. Blake goes to his friends and I stand by myself, feeling a little bit like my day of fame is over. Not sure I like that, actually. I mean, I don't like the attention, but I don't like nonattention even more. Tomorrow I'm bringing earbuds, even if I don't have a player to plug into. I can fake it.

I don't sit with Cami, even though she's sitting alone

like she's waiting for me. I want to, but there's the little matter of the asswipe, and I've decided I can't handle it, personally. I just can't. It's a stability thing. I have to pretend I don't like her, or I could get a little freaky. And I'm not going there.

At school, I see the dude everywhere, now that I know what he looks like. He even says hi to me once. He's in half my classes and my lunch hour.

I take my tray and go up to him like the ballsy homeless Ethan would do. "Hey," I say. "Can I sit?" He's bigger than me.

Asswipe shrugs. "Sure."

I eat a few bites in silence. Drink some milk. "I'm new," I say.

"You're that abducted kid."

"Right."

"Who abducted you? Was it, like, for a reward? Your parents loaded?" He's got this sincere look, like he doesn't even know he's asking stupid-ass questions.

"No . . . she just wanted a kid, I guess. Really bad."

He laughs loud at this, and other large guys join us and sit down quietly. "Sh'yeah. That's a pretty nutty thing to do, swiping somebody else's kid just because you want one. Was she a total loco?"

I look around nervously as the guys surround me. "I . . . I guess so. Heh."

"What a lunatic."

"Well, she wasn't that bad. I mean, she was nice to me."

"That's whack. Is she in jail now?"

I'm starting to feel uncomfortable. "Yeah, uh, no, she's still out there somewhere, probably on an abducting rampage." I take a bite of the brown meat product on my plate. "So," I say, changing the subject. "What's your name?"

He grins wide. "Lucky number thirteen, Jason 'J-Dog' Roofer."

"ROOOOOF," says the rest of J-Dog's posse.

I almost choke on my roll. Gracie would get along great with these guys—they're right at her level. "I'm, uh, Ethan. E-Dog."

The posse doesn't say anything, and J-Dog snorts again. "You'll know who I am by the end of the week. Basketball game Friday night. You're going. You sit at my table, that means you're one of my friends now. Right, guys?"

"I—I don't know," I say, and I shove the pasty mashed potatoes in my mouth and pray that I have enough saliva to swallow them. Getting a stomachache. I push my chair back. "Maybe. See you later."

"No, you're going. Everybody goes." He's still grinning. Like, nicely, though I keep waiting for him to beat the shit out of me. God.

I shrug and head over to the dishwashing station to chuck my tray.

After school they're there again, leaning against the bus and talking this time. J-Dog sees me and shouts, "Yo, little E-Dog!"

There's a guy like him in every school. "Roooof!" I say. I reach out and bump his waiting fist, and then I accidentally trip going up the steps into the bus on account of catching Cami's surprised look. I feel the rumble of panic laughter build up, but I hold it back. I have nothing to panic about. Nothing. Everything is exactly as it should be, and getting better every day.

Cami hops up the steps and flops into my seat with me. "So . . . how's it going at school?" The bus pulls away from the curb.

"Pretty good, most of it. Spent half the day testing so the teachers can figure out where to put me. I have more tests the rest of the week. Hope I can get out of some of the loser freshman classes." I'm actually kind of worried about this.

"You making any friends?"

"Besides J-Dog Roofer?" I try to hold back the sarcasm.

But she's defensive. "It's just a silly name to get the basketball crowd riled up. He doesn't even like it."

"What—I didn't say anything about J-Dog Roofer's name."

"You had a tone. Stop it."

"I did not. Why are you so defensive about your boy-friend?"

"I'm not!"

Her mouth is a frown and all of a sudden I just want to taste those pouty lips. I look at her eyes and she's glaring at me. I lock my eyes on hers and suddenly we're in a staring contest, neither of us willing to blink. But hers are like black holes. I'm sucked in.

Finally, I wet my lips and smile at her, and then I blink, giving up. She gives a reluctant grin back.

"You dork," she says.

I shrug and grin, shifting in the seat until our legs touch, and I pretend I don't notice. She doesn't move away. She pulls her iPod out of her coat pocket and offers me an earbud. And so we sit, thighs and shoulders touching, listening to some screamo crap.

When the middle schoolers get on the bus, Blake gives me a look, like he thinks I'm pathetic. I shrug and pull out some stupid forms I have to fill out, and then just rest and listen, eyes closed, picturing things the way I want them to be.

I go straight home this time, and Mama presents me with a cell phone. I dump my stuff in the bedroom, where Blake is spreading out his homework on his bed.

"Can you show me how to work this thing?" I ask.

"Seriously?"

"Yeah. I've never owned one."

Blake just looks at me like I'm a total fucktard. "What's your number?"

I point to it on the paper Mama gave me, and then he takes out his phone and starts punching buttons. I stare, totally intrigued. I move his stuff over, sit down, and watch him. "What are you doing?"

"Sending contacts to your phonebook. Mine, the landline, Dad's, Mama's. Gracie doesn't have one. You want Cami's, too? I have it."

"Ah . . . yeah."

He laughs and checks for more. When he's done, he shows me how to make calls and look up people and send text messages.

"Thanks."

"Sure." Blake turns back to his homework. "Your other . . . people. The abductor dudes. They didn't have cell phones?"

"Nope," I say. "And it was a woman. Eleanor." Her fake name comes out easily now.

Blake looks up. "Just a woman? What about the guys?"

"What guys?"

"The two guys in the car, that took you."

I stand up and shove the cell phone in my pocket. "I don't remember it. I don't know any two guys. So you're sure two guys were in the black car?" I feel my heart race.

"That's what I remember," he says. "I can see it. Passenger-side guy leans out the window, gives you something. You get in the backseat. I yell when the car drives away." He pauses. "I thought you were getting to do something I wasn't getting to do. I mean, I think I was too little to understand about getting in the car with strangers. Unlike you, who should have known."

I flop down on my bed and get my homework out, study guides for the rest of the testing I'll be doing this week. I ponder the new information from Blake and ignore the barb. "What are you working on?"

"Science."

After a minute of getting organized, I get a weird feeling and look up, and Blake is staring at me again. "What?"

Blake shakes his head. "I'm just trying to figure out why two guys would kidnap you and you'd end up with a woman. Did she hire them to do it or something?"

I sigh. "Blakey, I really don't know." But after I think about it a little more, I like that story. "Yeah, maybe," I say. "That makes sense." I move another piece of me into place. Close my eyes and memorize the picture of it.

For the English test prep I read some wacky Emily Dickinson poem over and over again, not really comprehending it. Thinking about Ellen . . . and about why I changed her name when I started talking about her.

She's really not such a bad person. Not as bad as J-Dog made her out to be. Even after what she did to me in Nebraska, and never coming back . . . I guess I still hope she doesn't get caught.

# CHAPTER 18

The days crawl along and I get through them, doing most of my homework and flirting a little, not too much. I've been here a week. It still feels weird. Sometimes I just have to go detox down in the basement, in my little cubby of boxes.

On Friday, J-Dog stakes me out and asks if I got a ticket to the stupid basketball game.

"No," I say. "I don't have anybody to go with."

"The whole junior class sits together. Get a ticket. You'll get to know some people."

"I don't have any money."

J-Dog looks around and spies somebody. "Hey, Zack, you got two bucks for my new friend Ethan? He needs a game ticket."

"Sure thing," Zack says. "Can do you one better. Here's mine. I'll go buy another one."

"That's what I'm talking about," J-Dog says.

I watch this all. I don't understand it, why these jocks are nice to me, but I take the ticket. "Why do you want me to go so bad?"

"Because we're hospitable here at Belleville High. And everybody—EVERYBODY—goes to see the J-Dog play. 'Specially my homies. I like you, little E-Dog. You're scrappy. And you're a survivor, man. Look at you, finding your way back home from that creepy woman. You're like a hero or a celebrity or something. You ever play hoops? You should."

I've never played basketball outside of shitty PE classes. I ignore the question. "I'll try to get a ride."

"You call the J-Dog if you need a ride. I'll have my people come get you. Okay? Just be there. Five-eight-six-J-Dog."

"Okay."

"Okay." J-Dog peers at me, apparently satisfied, and lets me go as the bell rings.

When we get home from school, Dad's already there. Mama's putting Gracie's hair in braids. "What's going on?" Blake asks. He grabs a granola bar from the cupboard and rips it open.

"We're going to the basketball game," Mama says.

"What?" Blake freezes, granola bar nearly to his mouth.

"You heard her," Gracie says. She sticks her nose in the air.

"We don't go to games. We never go anywhere," Blake says. I can tell he's got a bug up his butt, the way he's winding up.

"We're going to start now," Mama says. "We've got a child in high school, and it's my alma mater too, you know. It's something we should have been doing for a long time. A good family tradition."

"I'm not going," Blake says. "I'm not sitting with you."

"Yes, you are." Mama has a look in her eye I wouldn't want to go up against.

Blake shakes his head, incredulous, and stomps off to the bedroom. "Why not just torture me instead?"

I stay out of his way.

Ellen would call him a hothead.

It's snowing again. Inside the field house entryway, the floor is slick with filthy slush. Black carpets gush when you step on them, but the ones closer to the basketball courts are only damp. I wipe my shoes off and look around for familiar faces. There are people everywhere—students and families. It's like the major event of Belleville or something.

I see some of Cami's friends from the bus stop and the butterflies in my gut slow down a little bit. At least I know where to go.

I turn to Dad. "Is it cool if I sit with my, uh, friends?"

Dad looks alarmed. "Where?"

"Just right over there, Dad. I'll meet you here at this coatrack after the game."

"I—I don't know. Maria? What do you think?"

"What?" Mama says.

"He wants to sit with his friends."

Mama hesitates, but only for a second, and then she gives me a strained smile. "That's a great idea. Of course. When you're in high school, you have to. That's what I always did too. Junior section is there, isn't it?" She points.

I nod. "I'll meet you right here after the game. I'll be fine," I add. "I have my cell phone if you need me."

Blake stands there looking pissed, and Gracie just stares at all the people.

"Okay," Mama says. "Have fun. Don't miss out on the halftime show. It's usually pretty interesting."

"Right," I say, and I take off for the bleachers. It feels like everybody's watching me. I think I might puke, I'm so nervous. I climb up the steps between sections and see the guy, Zack, who gave me his ticket.

"Hey," I say uncertainly.

"Hey, new guy. Glad you made it. Told you everybody

comes to these. There's competitions between the classes."

"Yeah, okay," I say. I totally have to pee.

Zack and his friends shove down on the bench to make room, and I sit. There's a band playing, and everybody's shouting and talking. I can feel drum vibrations in my chest. It's kind of thrilling, actually. Zack hollers to the people down the row and I just sit and watch, trying to calm down.

The cheerleaders come out and start jumping around. One girl looks familiar, like she's in one of my classes. Math, I think. She's pretty. I think about being with her. God, I'd give anything to just hold a girl. It's been a long time—nobody wants to hold a homeless guy. It's like my skin is aching for it.

I watch the people coming up the bleacher steps, and then I see Cami. She climbs up and stops when she sees me. Breaks into a big smile.

"Hey!" she says, and sits down next to me. "Make room!" she yells, and smacks Zack on the head. Everybody shoves down. She puts her hand on my shoulder. "You'll be glad you came," she says in my ear.

I shiver with excitement. I'm already glad.

The game isn't nearly as exciting as being in the middle of a huge screaming crowd next to a girl you used to take baths with. I yell along with everybody when it comes time to compete for the juniors in the school spirit shout-off, but we take second place to the stupid loudmouth sophomores.

At one point I see my family, up in the first balcony above one basket. I think Dad's watching me. I don't wave because that would be dorky, even though I know he probably wants me to. It's so weird being here. Having a dad, a whole family like this. I'm almost overwhelmed for a second.

Halftime comes and I stand up. I really have to pee now. I lean down to let Cami know I'm going to hit the restroom, and she gets a funny look on her face. "No, don't—there will be a mad rush right now. Wait until third quarter starts and you'll be in and out in a minute."

I shrug and sit down again. And then the announcer guy comes onstage, near the pep band. He calls for attention and Cami grips my knee. I look down at her hand, then at her, and she's grinning huge.

"What the . . . ," I say.

The announcer is talking now, and the field house grows fairly quiet. He welcomes everybody and the lights dim a little. A large screen, hanging from the ceiling above the pep band, rolls down, and then the announcer says something that scares the crap out of me.

"Once there was a boy who disappeared from our fair city, snatched from his front yard, leaving no trace," he says in this awful overdramatic voice. My heart stops beating. "He was abducted, and the people of Belleville searched high and low for him. But he was gone, leaving Belleville, his neighbors, and especially his family mourning deeply over his loss." A film begins playing. My jaw drops open and I feel the heat start to creep up. "But now the community and KTRX-AM radio are so pleased to welcome Ethan De Wilde back home!"

The audience breaks out in applause and the people around me start clapping me on the back, and Cami's squeezing my knee and laughing, and I'm just staring, flabbergasted, horrified, so very horrified, when the makeshift film tribute begins.

And there I am, my second-grade picture splashed on the big screen, and then part of the news clip that Cami showed me, and another news clip from a different TV station that I hadn't seen before of people searching, and then a clip of me on some missing-and-wanted TV program, which nobody told me about ever, and I am feeling so sick I think I'm going to throw up right here, right in the bleachers, over the entire junior class of Belleville High.

But then the film ends, the lights go up, people are cheering, and the announcer, shouting over the noise, calls me to come down to the floor where he stands. And that starts me off in hysterics. The laughing. I know I look like a freak, and I can't catch my breath, and Cami's pulling me to my feet and dragging me down the steps, and then slowly everything gets eerily quiet and things start swaying around me and getting dim, and I'm cackling like a lunatic, gasping for air, tripping down the steps, when my knees give out. I plunge forward, feel my bursting bladder let go and my head hit hard on the wooden step.

Everything goes black.

# CHAPTER 19

When I come to, it's chaos. There are people all crowding around me. I blink, and somebody's mother, in a BHS hoodie, is looking down at me. "I'm a paramedic," she says. "You fainted. Can you hear me?"

"Yeah," I say. I'm out of breath and my head hurts. And I feel it—the clammy, quickly cooling wetness all down my jeans. "Oh, shit," I say. I close my eyes.

"I called an ambulance when I saw you go down. Keep your eyes closed, try to relax, and we'll get you out of here," she says. "Here comes the stretcher." She shields me from onlookers, and every once in a while she yells at them, "Stand back, we need room!"

"I pissed my pants."

"It happens. Your jeans are dark. Nobody can tell. It's

okay. What the hell were they thinking springing this on you, anyway? Did your parents know about this? I wasn't far away. You looked like you didn't know this was going to happen."

I don't answer. I don't know about my parents. But I think they are in on it. Why else would they suddenly start going to games when they never have before? Cami, definitely. She knew it was coming. Hell, so did J-Dog, I bet. That's why he forced me here. Plus, they probably tell each other everything. Jesus. I keep my eyes closed. I don't want to see any of them.

The other paramedics come. They put me on a stretcher and take me to the ambulance, and the woman with the sweatshirt stays by my side. I see Mama and Dad and Blake and Gracie fighting their way through the crowd, trying to get to me. Gracie's bawling.

The woman leans down and says in my ear, "You want anyone to come in the back here with you?"

My throat hurts. "No," I whisper. I turn my head, which is really pounding now.

"Meet us at the hospital," she barks at my family, and the other paramedics close the doors.

# CHAPTER 20

They examine me at the hospital. Concussion. Keep me there for observation overnight because they are worried about my brain bleeding, but it looks like I'm fine. Just a gigantic bump on my head. That, and my room smells like a urinal.

I think about what I have to face at school Monday. Everybody will know. I'm sure there was piss on the floor that had to be cleaned up. God.

Who does that to a person? I turn over onto my side, curl up, and stare at the wall, remembering it, how sick it made me feel. When I squeeze my eyes shut, the silent sobs come, and I have to grip my knees until it stops.

I think about how it was with Ellen. No matter how

much she neglected me, she never would have tried to humiliate me.

My parents come in the room and I pretend I'm asleep. I don't want to see anybody—I can't. Later I hear that Cami's there too, missing the end of J-Dog's game. I hope they lose. Sons of bitches.

The nurse comes in and shoos my parents out. She sits by the bed and asks how I feel.

"I'm okay," I say. "Headache."

"On a scale of one to ten, one being barely noticeable and ten being unbearable, how bad is it?"

"Four or five."

"Okay," she says. She writes it down. "Now, about the visitors."

"No more visitors. Just tell them I don't want to see anybody and they should all go home. I'll take a cab in the morning." I have absolutely no money.

She smiles. "I'm pretty sure they aren't going to leave. There's a little girl out there. Gracie. She thinks you're dead. Won't stop crying."

"My sister. You told her I'm not dead, right?"

"Of course! But she saw you on the stretcher with your eyes closed, being shoved into an ambulance. And that's all she knows."

I think about that. Feel that little bit of panic start in my gut. "Is this a trick to get them in here again?"

"No. You don't have to do anything. I just thought I'd tell you about the girl."

I rub my eyes and run my fingers gingerly through my hair.

Stupid little girl.

"All right," I say. "Just Gracie, nobody else. You bring her in here."

She comes up to the room walking on tiptoes and stops at the door. The nurse says, "It's okay. See? There he is. He's just got a sore head."

Gracie holds on to the doorframe and sniffs. Her cheeks are all splotchy red from crying. I wave, feeling stupid. Finally I ease up to a sitting position. "Come here, then," I say.

She shuffles in halfway.

"Come on."

She sidles up to the bed.

"Hi."

Her lip quivers. "Hi, Efan."

"You okay?"

She wrinkles up her nose. "Something's stinky."

I sigh. "Okay, that's enough, girlie. Go back out there and tell Mama and Dad to go home. I'll call tomorrow when I need a ride." I buzz the nurse.

"Cami's here too."

"Tell them all that I have to go to sleep now."

The nurse comes in. "Had enough for today, Ethan?" She gives me a look.

"Yeah. Can you just tell them I don't want to see any-body and they should just go home and get some sleep?" I hope they respect that, after what they did to me.

"Will do. Come on, Gracie."

Gracie obediently takes the nurse's hand. "Bye, Efan. See you tomorrow."

"Bye, Gracie. Stop crying now."

"Okay."

In the dark, I can't stop thinking about what happened and all the people who betrayed me. And I think maybe there's no other option.

I'm going to have to run.

# CHAPTER 21

They wake me up all night, every hour or two, I think. In the morning I walk over to the window and push the curtain aside. Snow. More and more snow here. So cold. I imagine what it's like living on the streets around here, and I shiver and turn away.

I guess things aren't as bad this morning as they felt last night.

In my mind, I come up with a list of demands. My own bedroom in the basement. Some privacy. And I'm not going to school. No way. Not going back there, not going to face them. I'll homeschool myself or just drop out. I'm sixteen, I can do whatever I want.

When the doc comes in and says I'm good to go, I don't have a choice. Not one that I'm willing to make, anyway, thanks to the snow. I call home.

"Hello?" Mama sounds worried.

"It's Ethan . . ."

"Honey, I'm so sorry," she says. "We didn't know it would be like that. Please let me explain."

I swallow hard and pinch the bridge of my nose. "Can you just bring me some jeans and pick me up?"

"I'll be there in fifteen minutes."

"Thanks." I hang up and stand in my hospital gown, my ass hanging out. My soiled jeans and boxers are in a plastic bag and ready to go. It's mortifying.

Mama arrives with the jeans, bringing clean boxers, too, and my coat, which I guess I left on the bleachers. I change in the bathroom as Mama signs the final papers, and we're gone.

In the car, the only sound is the massive whoosh of the heater. I stare out the window, willing Mama with my silence to come up with something that makes me not hate her.

"I got a call yesterday morning," she says. "The school principal said that a group of basketball players had come up with the idea to just say a little 'welcome home' to you at the game. Friends of yours."

I snort.

"Well, that's what they told me. Jason Roofer—you know him, obviously. That boy Cami goes with. He's a nice boy. Very thoughtful. It was Jason's idea and he approached Al, the radio announcer who always announces our games and interviews Jason now and then. Jason asked Al to say a little something at halftime from the booth to welcome you back. That's all it was going to be, according to Jason—I promise. It sounded like just a small thing. They invited us to come too, but asked us to keep it a secret. Jason wanted you to be surprised."

"No kidding."

"I had no idea Al was going to make such a scene and dig up all that footage. But I guess in a small town like this, people jump on any little bit of celebrity they can claim, you know? Al obviously went way too far with his enthusiasm. It was horrible—Ethan, it was horrible for us, too, for Blake especially, and for Gracie, who didn't understand any of it. It was terrible to see all of that again. I can't believe he did it. I'm furious. And Al has heard from me. He apologized."

She sounds sincere.

"I'm not going back there," I say.

Mama is silent as she pulls into the garage. She turns the car off. "Cami and Jason feel terrible."

I ponder this, but sorrys can't erase anything. "I'm not going to talk to those guys, and I'm not going back there.

I'm quitting school. And," I say, feeling bold, "I want my own room in the basement."

Mama just looks at me, her eyes sad, and doesn't say anything. Doesn't say no. Not to any of it.

When we get home, I go straight downstairs in the dark and sit in my spot against the wall, among the boxes of a stranger. You'd almost think that after a hit to the head like that, I'd get my memory back. But no such luck.

# CHAPTER 22

From my basement location, I can just barely hear Mama and Dad talking somewhere above my head. I open the heater vent all the way and I don't have to strain very hard at all to listen. Dad's voice gets louder and I can tell he's mad about what I told Mama. My demands. They start arguing. I don't like it.

Upstairs, everybody but Gracie is being weird about things, but we are forced by a blizzard to hang out all together at home the rest of the weekend.

Dad tells me he's sorry about what happened. Blake acts like I did something wrong to him. Cami comes to the door covered in snow to see how I'm doing but I won't go talk to her, so after a while of talking to Mama, she leaves.

And then J-Dog calls. I watch Mama on the phone,

talking to him, telling him I'm not up to talking quite yet. Lying for me. I get a little twinge in my chest, like love or whatever.

If Mama tries to hug me now, I'll let her, I guess. But she doesn't.

Gracie sits by me on the couch. And I realize that I don't despise her like I thought I would. I kept expecting her to be like all the six-year-old girls I saw at the zoo and out shopping with their parents, whining and begging and chomping on gum, and I never thought I'd like one of them. Gracie is definitely annoying sometimes, but she's also kind of smart.

We're watching some stupid sitcom marathon. I don't like it, but that's what's on. It doesn't matter anyway, because Gracie won't shut up about the stuff she saw last night, about the news clips and the missing boy and how I was kidnapped. She's completely fascinated by it, not scared at all. Weird kid.

"Why did you get in the car with those guys?" she asks. The question of the month.

I sigh. "I don't know, Gracie. I don't remember doing it."

"Where did they take you?"

"I'm not sure. I don't remember them. All I remember is Eleanor."

"Who's that?"

"She's the woman who acted like my mama while I was gone."

"She wasn't as nice as Mama." She says it as a matter of fact.

I think about that. "No," I say. "You're right."

"Then how come did you—?"

"Gracie, I don't know. I don't remember. Okay?" I'm getting frustrated now. "I look at pictures, and people tell me stories, and sometimes I think I can remember things. Little bits of things. But so far, that's not very much."

"How old were you?"

"A little older than you."

"I would remember everybody," she says, and I have nothing to defend myself with. Gracie tilts her head and looks at me. "Does your head still hurt?"

"Yes."

"That's not cool."

I laugh. "No. It's not. I think if we stop talking, it will feel better."

She shrugs, and as the snowy, late-afternoon light turns dusky, she leans up against me and links her arm with mine, and I smile at her. Later, she crawls into my lap and we just sit like that, like I've got this little warm, fuzzy-headed package in my arms, and we watch TV until the marathon ends.

# CHAPTER 23

In bed at night, Blake and I don't talk, we just listen to Mama and Dad arguing in their room next door. Sometimes I catch words. They're talking about money, and adding a bedroom. And about me and school. Mama's in my court all the way.

"Good job," Blake says. The sarcasm is obvious.

"What?"

"You did it again, and you've only been here, what, ten days?"

"What are you talking about?" I don't like this. Blake's been too quiet lately. He hid out in the bedroom all day today. Playing depressing music.

"Got them fighting again. Like after you left."

I roll over and stare at the wall in the dark. This room is so tiny, I'm feeling claustrophobic. I can't stand being in here with him baiting me like that.

I try to like him, try to be nice, but he's got such a huge chip on his shoulder about me. I start to wonder if he'll ever get over it.

"You were four years old," I say. "How can you even remember the fighting?"

"You were seven. How can you *not* remember being abducted?"

"Lay off."

"You."

I clench my jaw, fuming silently. He can't stand not having the last word. I let him have it. This time.

Mama and Dad's arguing fades, and I fall into one of those hard sleeps where, when you wake up, you don't know where you are.

In the morning they go to church, but Mama lets me stay home. "My head still hurts," I say. That excuse won't work much longer. But I'm worried. Worried they're going to try to make me go to school tomorrow. I end up wandering the house, listening for where the floorboards creak.

It's nice having the house to myself. I snoop around, looking at things without somebody watching me. I like that. I do. It's the most at home I ever feel here. And it's cool that they trust me not to take anything. I wouldn't do that. Nothing like that.

After a while I get bored, so I go downstairs and picture where my bed will be once I get a new bedroom. There's no way I'm staying with Blake. I'd rather sleep on the floor down here than do that.

When they get home from church, Dad tells me to get my coat. We're going to the lumberyard to get wood for my new room. Way to go, Mama, or church, or whatever it was that convinced him. Probably church, since he wasn't budging with Mama last night. Go, Jesus.

It's sort of cool to be out with Dad, just him and me. I never had a dad. I mean, not that I can remember. We grab lunch first, and we talk. About sports and the news, which I know nothing about, and about what I want to be, what I want to do when I get out of high school.

That stops me. I haven't spent much time thinking about what I want to be. More like who I am. I'm stuck in the past, trying to figure out who I am, what I came from, before I can know what I want to be. But Dad gets me thinking. We don't discuss school, but I know that's why he's asking. And I realize I have no interests. I'm a chameleon, just blending in. No goals but survival.

•   •   •

We haul the lumber into the garage, move a ton of junk around in the basement to clear the space, and then we build the frame. I have no idea how to do this. But Dad teaches me. He makes Blake help us, too, which is actually okay, because Blake pretty much wants me out of his room too. Finally, we agree on something. And he seems to know a little bit about what he's doing, so it goes faster.

It's evening and I'm starving and sweaty when I hear the steps creak. I look, and there's Cami, coming downstairs. My stomach twists and I grab my T-shirt, put it back on. "What are you doing here?" I ask.

Dad looks up. "Hi, Cami," he says, and then he glances at his watch. "I'm going to go out for some burgers, guys. Back in twenty minutes, maybe thirty if the roads are really bad. Supposed to start blowing tonight. Blake, did you do your homework?"

"No," Blake mumbles.

"Why don't you get started on that?" Dad wipes his hands, and then heads up the steps.

"Bye, Mr. De Wilde," Cami calls out.

"Nice to see you, Cami." Dad closes the door at the top of the stairs and it's quiet again. Blake doesn't leave.

"What are you doing here?" I ask Cami again, not very nicely.

"I came to talk to you. I want to say I'm sorry for what happened."

"Who let you in?"

"Gracie."

"You manipulated a little kid?"

"She answered the door and said come in."

Blake is smirking in the corner, enjoying this.

I turn to him. "Don't you have homework to do? Or do I have to tell Dad you're being a dickhead?"

Blake scowls, but then, after a moment, he saunters off upstairs.

"Look, Ethan," Cami says. "The whole thing blew up. Jason didn't—"

"Who's Jason? You mean the J-Dog?" I can't stop the sarcasm. But I'm embarrassed all over again, thinking about what happened. And I don't want to talk about J-Dog.

"Yeah, that's his name. You knew that."

I shrug. Does it matter?

"Your mom said you want to quit school over this."

"So?"

"Why would you do that?"

"Because school sucks. And so does everybody who thinks it's funny to humiliate me in public."

"Ethan!" Cami wrings her hands. "That is so stupid. You are making this into something so much bigger than it is."

This ticks me off. "I'm thinking maybe I don't need to be anywhere near friends like you."

Her jaw drops. She steps back. I can see the shock, the hurt, in her eyes. I went too far. Fuck.

I went too far and now I'm going to lose her. I press my lips together to stop the hysterics that threaten to bubble up. And then I do it.

I step in. Reach my fingers through her hair and pull her close and I'm kissing her. Hard and sweet. Her lips are so soft, so delicious. And she's kissing me back, I think. For a second.

One second. And it's over. Then she freezes and whispers, "What are you doing?" Whether to me or to herself, I don't know. She pulls away and I can see her eyes wide, scared, and I let her go. I do. I just let her go.

She runs. Up the stairs, two at a time. Slams the door behind her. And my feet are glued to the floor.

God. She drives me insane. I hop up on the pool table, shove the balls aside, and lay back before they all bounce off the bumpers and come back to hit me. I stare up at the light fixture until I start seeing black spots everywhere. Knowing I messed it all up.

When I hear Dad come back, I go upstairs to clean up and change my shirt. And when we all sit around the table to eat, Blake has to go and act like an ass.

He's got a piece of paper and he's peering at Mama and Dad, then Gracie. And he's making notes.

"What are you writing?" Gracie asks, eyes narrow. "Don't look at me. Mama!"

Blake snarls at her. "It's my science assignment. Sheesh."

Mama tilts her head. "What is it?"

"I have to chart everybody's eye color in my family. We just started genetics."

"Ahh," Dad says. "I remember that. Good old eighth-grade science. Dominant, recessive genes . . . good times." He takes a bite of his burger.

But I'm staring at Blake's chart.

He's got Mama, Dad, himself, and Gracie on the chart. Not me. He's not including me in his family. He's not checking my eye color.

Jerk.

Blake puts his paper on top of his notebook, like he's done with the assignment, and starts eating.

I look over at Mama to see if she noticed Blake didn't include my eyes. But she's oblivious, helping Gracie open a ketchup packet.

I glare at Blake and point to the paper, and he gives me this innocent "Oh, I forgot about you!" look. He thinks it's a big joke, I can tell.

Well, it's not. I start to breathe hard.

I'm not going to lose it here in front of him. But this kind of little shit—this is what kills me, you know? It's so stupid, but I've got this thing, this . . . this already broken *thing* cracking into more pieces inside me. And it hurts so bad, right here in my chest, right inside my ribs. Because what the hell kind of thing is that to do to somebody? I shove my chair back and flee to the basement. In the dark. Ignoring the commotion I've just started.

In one simple move, Blake makes me feel like I'm not even a part of this family.

I hear some major yelling, more than I've ever heard here before, and I can tell Mama and Dad have figured it out. Blake's getting mauled, and I'm glad.

Later, Dad sends him downstairs with his stupid chart and he flips on the light. I think about closing my eyes so he can't even check, but that would be doing exactly what he's doing.

He's pissed off, I can tell by the way he's digging his pen into the paper. He charts my green eye color next to everyone else's: brown for Mama, Dad, and Gracie. Blue for him. I turn away when he's had his look. He stomps back up the stairs.

Nobody else comes down. But I can hear Mama and Dad fighting in their room above me again. Dad's going to make me go back to school. Ugh. I want to pound my head against the wall.

Maybe I'm just not meant to be here, not wired to fit in anymore, after all these years away. I decide to sleep on the floor down here, down where it's safe and I don't have to deal with them. Turn off the light, close the ceiling vent so I don't have to listen anymore, and pull the quilt over me. I start thinking about Blake, and about Cami, and how I just did the same thing to her that Blake did to me. But then I fucked it up even worse. At least Blake didn't try to kiss me after stabbing me in the gut.

I reach for my phone and send Cami a text message, telling her I'm sorry for what I said. That I was wrong and she was right. And that I didn't mean to kiss her. I shouldn't have done it.

She doesn't reply.

Maybe, in the morning, I'll run.

# CHAPTER 24

A loud whisper wakes me up. "Efan!"

I grunt, lift my head, and peer through one eye. Gracie is in her pajamas, dancing like she has to pee. "What?"

"Snow day! No school."

I let my head fall again. But I'm relieved. Another crisis averted, at least temporarily. And there's no way I can run away, not in this weather.

Gracie keeps dancing and looking around wildly.

"Why are you hopping around like that? Because of the snow day? I thought you liked school."

She looks over her shoulder swiftly, eyes big. "I hate the basement. There's bugs and momsters down here."

"Mmm, bugs and momsters. I eat the bugs during the night instead of potato chips. Crunchy."

She grins, so sweet. "What about the momsters?"

I struggle to a sitting position and wrinkle my nose. "Nah. Too gooey."

She laughs and hops over and right into my lap, folding her toes up so nothing is touching the floor. She squeaks once, like she's a little bit scared of things, but she stops bouncing around.

I look at her, and she looks up at me. I can see the kid adores me. And I have no idea why. I wrap the blanket around her. "I won't let the momsters get you," I say. I pull *Where's Waldo?* out of a nearby box and we look at it together.

Mama comes down after a while with a breakfast tray. She sets it down and hops onto the pool table, across from us. She has a little smile on her face. She likes that at least two of us are getting along, I think.

"Did you sleep all right down here?" she asks. "I was worried about you."

"It was fine. Better than being in the room with that jerk."

"Ethan," Mama says, and Gracie echoes in the same reprimanding tone, "Efan."

"Well, it's true."

"It's hard for Blake," Mama says. "He had a tough time while you were gone."

"And that's my fault? Are you going to blame me for going with those guys, too?"

Mama just looks at me. "No, of course not."

I shrug. It seems pretty obvious that Blake's a jerk, then, since he *is* blaming me, but I'm not going to press it. I pick up a bagel and spread some cream cheese on it, still balancing Waldo on my knee.

"So," she says, "Ethan. We need to talk about school."

"Snow day today, no school," Gracie says. She bounces in my lap.

"Yes, today. But tomorrow, if there's not a snow day, everybody needs to go to school again. Like usual."

I frown and shake my head slightly. I'm not going. I feel the panic rev in my gut. "I don't think that's a good idea," I say.

"Why? Because of what happened Friday night at the game?"

Duh, I want to say, but I am earnest. "Seriously, I just don't think I can handle that right now, Mama. This is hard enough."

"Dad says you need to go to school and that's final."

"Dad doesn't understand," I say, and I can feel that panic in my stomach come out as a whine in my voice. I set the bagel down.

Mama presses her lips together. She's hesitating. "Well, we have our appointment this afternoon with

Dr. Frost. We can talk about it then."

I let the book drop, and Gracie scrambles with her jelly toast to get it, spilling a glob of grape on my bare knee. "Watch it," I say, and it sounds mean. I see her sad face as I wipe it up, and even though I'm still mad, I feel bad.

I don't want to go to a shrink. I don't want him tricking me into talking about Ellen.

Unless, maybe, there's a chance I can get him to back me up. Convince him I can't go to school. I sigh. "Okay," I say. "Fine."

It takes us forty minutes to go five miles to the other side of town in this ridiculous snow. I'm hoping there'll be another snow day tomorrow. Buy some more time. When we get to Dr. Frost's office, Mama fills out a bunch of paperwork, and then we get called in. My hands are quivering and my stomach hurts. I don't want to be here.

Until I see Dr. Frost.

She's maybe thirty, if that. She's tall, and she's got this gorgeous flowing hair, and this rack. Jesus. I'm so distracted I don't even hear what she says.

"Ethan?"

"Uh, hi."

"I asked if you want your mother to stay in the room, or should she wait in the waiting room?"

I start fantasizing about what could happen if Mama

left us alone. And then I desperately start pinching myself. Thinking about dead puppies. Grandma De Wilde. "She can stay," I manage to say as I pull out my leg hair through my pockets.

That does it. Having Mama stay in the room is definitely enough to put things back in order.

Dr. Frost talks about herself a little bit, and how she likes to conduct the fifty-minute session, and then she asks me some easy questions—name, date of birth, age at the time of abduction, crap like that. She seems to know some things about me already.

And then she says, "Tell me about Eleanor." She sits back and shuts up.

I cross my legs. "I don't know, like, what do you want to know?"

"You lived with her until she abandoned you in Nebraska?"

"Yes."

"Did you like her?"

I glance at Mama and shift in my seat. Mama stays quiet and looks at her folded hands in her lap. "She was all right."

"Did you call her Eleanor?"

"Sometimes," I say. It's a lie. That's not even her name.

"Something else?"

I stare at the floor.

Nobody moves.

"Does it really matter?" I ask finally.

Dr. Frost smiles and changes the subject. "How did you feel when Eleanor left you at the youth home in Nebraska?"

I feel that stirring, and it's not the good kind. "It was fine. It *is* fine. Because that's what helped me find my real family." The words spill out of my mouth like sawdust.

"Yes," Dr. Frost says. "Still, at the time, you didn't remember you had another family. So it must have been a little bit hard. Unless Eleanor treated you badly."

"She wasn't bad." I say it too fast. Mama glances at me. "She wasn't bad to me. She didn't abuse me or anything. We just . . . we had a hard life."

Dr. Frost leans forward and doesn't speak.

It's quiet again, and I feel pressure to continue. I try to think of something that will satisfy them. Something big. The minutes are creeping by. I start sweating. "She was an escort," I say. "You know. She hung out with . . . men. For pay. I called her by her first name because she didn't want anybody to think she was old enough to have a kid my age. She pretended she was my older sister and said our parents were dead." I pause, my mouth dry. "She got bigger tips that way."

Dr. Frost nods. "What else?"

I groan and lean my head against the wall. "Sheesh.

Nothing. That's all. That's all there is. Then she got too old-looking and used up. She couldn't get work anymore and had to get rid of me."

Dr. Frost pauses. And then asks, "Are you mad at her?"

"I don't know." Hell yes, I am.

"Why do you think she abducted you, Ethan?"

I've thought about this a lot over the past year, once I realized what had really happened to me. But I knew. I know. "Because she couldn't be pregnant. You can't be pregnant and have that job, you know. That's what I think."

"But she wanted a kid?"

"I think she just wanted a kid, yeah. I think she was just real lonely. And she wanted a bigger kid, like I was. I could feed myself, take care of myself when she was out, you know?" I'm just going with it now, but it feels right. It does. I think that's probably the way it was with Ellen.

"She left you alone a lot?"

"No. Well, I mean, in the evenings and during the night when I was just sleeping anyway. She was working."

"Did Eleanor ever abandon you before Nebraska?"

I don't like this question. I chuckle softly for a minute, and then it gets louder, and I feel the hysterics coming up my chest, my throat. I hold them down. "Like, not forever. Ha-ha-ha. Of course not." I laugh again, thinking how absurd it is. How ridiculous. And this time, the laughter is caught there, not stopping, not softening. I bend forward and move around, trying to interrupt whatever the fuck it is that keeps it going.

Mama looks concerned. I wave her off.

"For a short time? Did she ever leave you for a few days? A week?" Dr. Frost asks.

I shrug in answer to her question and raise a hand to let her know I can't speak, not right now. The laughter comes in a rough pattern, and I try to think of a song that would go to the beat of it. I don't want to talk about it anymore, anyway. I just want to go home, go down to my basement, and finish my bedroom. Stay in there.

Mama stands up and comes over, holds my shoulders. "Are you okay? Do you need help?"

It's much worse than the time after the TV interview. I shake my head and the hysterical laughter won't stop. It grows. I stand up and see Mama's frightened look. She's obviously not sure what to think.

I'm fine! I want to tell her. I'm fine! I hold my forefinger up to Dr. Frost, who doesn't seem alarmed at all.

"Try some deep breaths if you can," Dr. Frost says.

I try. But it's like laughter asthma. Once you start going, it's hard to bring it back down. Tears are running down my face now, and Mama's hovering, and finally she just hugs me so tight and rubs my back, shaking right along with me, and whispers to me, over and over again.

"It's okay, sweetie. It's okay."

What it is, is fucking embarrassing.

We drive home in the early snowy darkness, Mama leaning over the steering wheel, concentrating on not crashing. "We're going back for family counseling on Thursday. All of us. Okay?"

I shrug. I have no control anyway; why bother fighting it?

"Do you know how to drive?" she asks suddenly. "Did you ever learn?"

"No."

"Do you want to? It would be so convenient to have another driver in the house. If you're interested, that is."

My eyes widen. "Yeah," I say. "I think that would be awesome."

"Winter's the best time to learn," she says. "If you can drive in messes like this, you can drive in anything. I'll sign you up for a class tomorrow, okay?"

"Okay." I like that. And that reminds me. "What about school? You saw me in there," I say. I start blushing. It's so fucking embarrassing. "That's what'll happen at school when they start making fun of me. And once that happens, I'll be branded a freak for life. Seriously, Mama. I'll never hear the end of it. That's why I can't go. Plus," I add, "I know I'm going to get stuck in a bunch of freshman classes because I missed so much school, and all my friends are juniors. It sucks."

Mama's quiet. We inch along the road. And she says quietly, almost to herself, "I don't know, Eth."

When we finally get home, Mama stops me on the step as we go inside, and puts her hand on my coat sleeve. "Don't say anything. Let me handle this one," she says. And then she smiles and goes in.

I feel a surge of warmth toward her and, at the same time, new energy in my weary body. After having to fight every battle for myself for so everlastingly long, it's such a relief to have her. I finally have an ally.

"Thanks, Mama," I whisper, but she's already humming in the kitchen, getting ready for whatever's next.

# CHAPTER 25

Dinner is more awkward than ever.

"We're all going to family counseling on Thursday," Mama announces, and that sets the pace for the rest of the evening.

"What?" Blake says. His eyes are blazing.

"You said we never go anywhere as a family," Dad says. "Well, here's our chance."

"No way. I'm not going." Blake throws his fork at his plate. It sticks in his mashed potatoes with barely a sound.

I think he sees me smirk. I can't help it. He's so amusing, getting upset about such little things.

"Shut up, Ethan."

"Hey, I said nothing," I say. "Touchy."

"Back off!"

I tsk. "Sounds like you could use a little counseling session all to yourself."

"Boys," Dad says, pushing his chair back to let us know he means it. I think he might be a little nervous about having to break us up if we start fighting.

I look at Gracie and she's eating happily. She sees me looking at her and she squinches her eyes shut in a long blink. She's still working on the wink thing. She thinks she's doing it, though, which is enough to crack me up just a little again.

Blake hauls off and slugs me in the arm.

I shove my chair back and get this huge rush of heat boiling up in my head. I want to get right up in his face and scream at the top of my lungs. My body reacts before I can think, and within two seconds, I've got Blake around the throat with one hand, pinning him against his chair, my other fist back and ready to pound the jerk in the face.

Mama screams. "Stop it!"

And that stops me. I look at Blake, his little round face, his usually icy blue eyes now filled with fear, staring back at me. I lower my fist and let go of his neck, shake out my hand.

As soon as I let go, Blake flies out of his chair, nearly wipes out as he runs down the hallway to his room. He slams the door and yells something unintelligible.

I quickly pick up my chair and set it upright, unable to

look at Mama. I feel like I let her down. And everybody else just sits there, shocked. I don't think they're used to family dinners like this.

Gracie breaks the silence. I can see her eyes tearing up. "That was scary," she says. Her lip quivers. And then she starts crying.

Fuck.

"He punched me," I say, defending myself, and I feel like I'm babbling, but I have to say something. I have to explain. "He punched me first, like, totally out of the blue. I didn't hurt him. I didn't even laugh at him." And now I'm scared too. I rub my sore shoulder as Mama and Dad look at each other, silently discussing with their eyes what to do next.

"Stay put," Dad says calmly. He and Mama get up to go talk privately, leaving their food, and it's just me and Gracie left at the table.

She looks at me, all blubbery and scared.

"I'm sorry, Gracie. I didn't hurt him, okay? He startled me when he punched me and I just reacted. I'm sorry you're scared."

She just sits there, sad-faced.

A minute later, Blake's door opens wide and he starts throwing shit out into the hallway. All my stuff—my clothes, my backpack, my shoes. He's cussing, yelling crazy things.

Gracie covers her ears. And I can hear Dad coming.

I look at Gracie and shake my head, pushing my chair back. "Sorry, kid," I say. "I gotta go." And I feel bad. I do.

I slip out to the mudroom, grab my coat and hat, shove my feet in my boots, and I'm out the door.

# CHAPTER 26

From the street, I glance up at the big picture window, and there's Gracie, nose pressed against it, her little hands cupped around her eyes, peering out at me. The snow is coming down hard, and there's at least six fresh inches on the roads since the last snowplow came through this afternoon. I'm worked up enough to not be freezing quite yet, but I know I won't make it out here for long.

Not to mention, I still don't really know my way around. But I do know there's a gas station nearby. I head that way. Maybe I can hang out there for a while.

My thighs are nearly numb by the time I get there, but I manage to feel the vibration of my cell phone in my pocket. I'm still not used to that. Anyway, I figure it's Mama. Gracie would have told them by now.

But it's not Mama.

It's not Blake, or Dad.

It's a text from Cami.

*What r u doing?*

My thumbs are numb. And I'm really slow at this. Plus, the guy at the counter is giving me the hairy eyeball.

*nothing just wandering around*

It takes me a long minute to type it, and my nose is dripping. I shove the phone back into my pocket and pretend to look at milk in the refrigerator case.

In a ridiculously short amount of time, she replies.

*we need 2 talk*

I move to the chip aisle, staying in plain sight of the clerk so he doesn't freak out. I write back:

*I'm coming over, k?*

And I don't wait for her reply. I take off out the door, not too fast, so I don't look suspicious. On the way to Cami's, working against the snow and wind, my phone buzzes again. It's Dad. I don't want to answer, but I know they'll keep calling. They're freaking out, I'm sure.

"Hey, Dad."

"Ethan, where are you? Are you all right?"

"I'm fine. I'm just out for a bit. Taking a walk."

He's quiet, and I picture him, working his jaw.

"Where? We need to know where you are."

"I'm fine, Dad." I'm breathing hard, running to get to Cami's.

"Ethan, come home this instant. Or you're grounded."

I'm walking up Cami's driveway now, and I see her looking out the window, behind the curtains. "Dad, seriously. It's what, like seven thirty? Are you kidding me?"

"Ethan," he says, and even with the wind whistling around my head, I can hear his voice change to pleading. "Please come home. Your mother is very worried about you."

I shake my head and stomp off my boots on Cami's step. She opens the door. "Tell Mama I'm sixteen, not seven. Gotta go." I wipe the snow off my coat and hat as much as I can, and then I step inside.

Cami's not smiling.

Neither am I.

# CHAPTER 27

"Hi." I stand there in her entryway like an idiot.

"I said don't come over." Cami folds her arms over her chest.

"Sorry. I was on the phone. I must have missed that. Besides, you were watching out the window for me."

"Yeah, so I could tell you to leave."

I take off my hat and gloves. Unzip my coat. "Please don't make me leave. If I go home now, the terrorists win."

She tries not to laugh. "Was that your dad on the phone?"

"Yeah. They're treating me like I'm still seven. I can't go anywhere without them knowing where I am. They're currently threatening to ground me if I don't come home immediately."

"Ah," Cami says. She's eyeing me.

"Plus I need to thank your mother for the cookies from a couple weeks ago."

"They were brownies."

"Right." I smile as sweetly as I can. "Please?"

She steps back, shaking her head but waving her hand at the coat hooks. "Fine," she mutters.

I go inside and spend a few minutes with Cami's parents, catching up. Which means they tell me things I used to do and I smile and nod and pretend to be delighted about playing Easy-Bake Oven and Barbies with Cami. And then we go downstairs and hang out in the rec room. It's really nice and cozy down here, kind of like how I'd want our house to be.

Cami flops into a chair, leaving me the couch. She's not taking any chances.

"So," she says coolly. "You want to explain what the hell you were doing, kissing me?"

"Uh . . . ," I say. "I was being an ass."

"Seriously."

"Seriously being an ass, yes. I'm sorry."

"A big, big, gigantic ass."

"Yes. That." I nod.

She seems satisfied. "I'm not going to tell Jason, in case you're wondering."

It sounds like a threat, and I'm not sure I like it. "Okay, good," I say. "Then I won't tell him you kissed me back."

She explodes. "I did not!"

I smile. I know she did. That's all I need for now.

She relaxes a little. "You know," she says, as if she's suddenly remembered something, "that's not the first time you kissed me."

I sit up. "No?"

"You kissed me when we were six."

"See, I was a smart kid."

"Well, you sort of didn't have a choice."

I cock my head to the side. "I'm listening . . ."

"Jeremy Winger's big sister tricked you and me into going inside their dog pen to feed Spotty, and then she slammed the door and locked us in there."

"Jeremy," I say, thinking. "Did we call him Jermy? Like germs?"

Cami frowns. "I don't think so."

"Oh." So much for that almost-memory. "Anyway . . ."

"So, yeah, then she said she wouldn't let us out unless we kissed."

"I like her."

Cami props her bare feet on the coffee table. Her toenails are painted purple. "Stop it. It was horrible. There were tons of bees in there."

"Was I a good kisser back then already?"

"Shut up."

I stare at her toes for a minute, and then I look over at her face. "Aren't your feet freezing?"

She shrugs. "Sort of."

I get off the couch, move her legs, and slide under them so I'm sitting on the coffee table and her feet are in my lap. I wrap my arms around them, hold them to my chest. And then I give her my most innocent smile.

She raises her eyebrow suspiciously but lets me stay like that, and we talk about all kinds of things. Like what happened at dinner tonight with Blake, and which Barbie doll was my favorite, and what might happen when I finally make my way home.

One kiss was definitely not enough.

After a while, Cami's mom yells down the stairs. "Ethan, are you still here?"

"Yes, ma'am," I say. Cami's toes are toasty warm now.

"Your mother's on the phone wondering if you're here, and she wants you to come home now."

I roll my eyes and Cami cringes in sympathy. "Thanks," I call out. "Tell her I'll be home in a few minutes."

I stand up and set Cami's feet gently on the floor,

and then I offer her a hand and pull her out of the chair. "Thanks for forgiving me," I say.

She gives me a hug. "How could I not forgive my long-lost BFF?"

It's not where I want it to be. But I'll take it. For now.

# CHAPTER 28

The wind has stopped and the snowplows are out, throwing the snow impossibly high along the sides of the roads. It feels like I'm in a tunnel, walking down the street. Mama said earlier that if the plow trucks make it to the neighborhoods, school will be open tomorrow. And my mind turns back to that old worry. I squinch my eyes shut. My eyeballs feel frozen.

When I get home, I find my parents in the living room, pretending like crazy that they aren't worried, like they have it all together, but the curtains are still open wide, even though it's long after dark.

Blake is nowhere to be found, and Gracie's probably asleep in bed already. I sit down in the chair across from the couch, where Mama sits.

"Hey," I say. I'm so uncertain. Are they mad at me about dinner? Do they think I'm just a troublemaker, like Blake does? And are they really going to ground me for not coming home right away? I think about making a joke, but then think better of it and just keep my mouth shut.

They're quiet, just sitting there, looking at me, and it worries me. It does. It's probably some parenting technique or something. Whatever it is, it's working. I shift in my chair and clasp my hands to keep from fidgeting.

Finally, Dad speaks. "We're really upset with you for running off."

Mama says, "It's not safe out there. You wandering around in the dark—I was very worried."

I close my eyes and count to five so I don't mess this up.

But they aren't done.

"And what you did to Blake is unacceptable," Dad says. "I know you've had some rough times, and I know you probably learned how to fight on the street, but in this house you are with family and we don't act that way."

Ugh. I can't believe this. "Blake punched me first," I say as quietly as I can.

"Don't worry about Blake. We've taken care of him. That's not your job," Mama says.

I can feel it coming. This is such bullshit. And I know I've lost my chance at getting out of school. There's no way Mama will talk Dad into anything now.

"I'm sorry," I say. Seething inside.

Mama stays on point. "If it happens again, Ethan, well . . . I'm not sure what we're going to do, but violence in our home is not acceptable, and whatever punishment we decide, it'll be harsh. So just don't. Clear?"

"Yes."

"Now, about school tomorrow," Dad says.

My heart sinks.

"You're going."

Fuck. I lean forward in my chair, put my elbows on my knees. Bury my face in my hands so they don't see my reaction. So they don't see me shaking. So they don't see the stupid, hot tears.

In the morning, I get up from my makeshift bed in the basement, put on my clothes, eat breakfast, and get on the bus, ignoring the looks. And ignoring Blake. It's easy—he ignores me, too. I sit with Cami, but for the life of me, I can't focus on our conversation. My chest is so tight, it makes my breath raspy. I just stare at the seatback in front of me.

Once we're at school, I get off the bus.

And I start walking. Away.

I can't do it. I can't go in there, face all those people. Be laughed at, humiliated. Sent to all those freshman classes when I should be a junior. Look J-Dog in the eye, or see Cami with him, or get one single pity glance or one inkling of a mention of pissing my pants—I swear I'll punch anybody who does that.

And, I've been told, that is unacceptable.

So that leaves me with no choice.

I quit.

# CHAPTER 29

I spend the day wandering, and by afternoon, I'm cold and starving. I stare at the mom-and-pop diner a couple of blocks from school, smelling the grease, and my mouth waters. But I don't have any money. I walk farther and stop when I see a Burger King bag on the side of the road. It's not moving in the breeze. I think about seeing what's in it. I do. But I fucking can't do that again. I turn down a residential street and keep walking. Kick the crap out of a trash can instead. The lid rolls out into the street and a car has to go around it. I walk to the end of the block, and then jog back to get it. Put it back on the can.

Wandering around all day, I've got to keep moving or I freeze. I walk a bunch of miles, all in squares so I don't get lost. Nobody notices, nobody stops me or asks what I'm doing. I'm just invisible.

When my phone starts vibrating in my pocket, I ignore it along with the fear in my gut, and I just head back to school to catch the bus home. I don't know what I'm going to do. I really don't.

I hop on the bus before the last bell rings, before everybody else boards, and sit by the window watching the floodgates open. Cami and J-Dog come walking out together, holding hands, and I want to kill him. I shrink down in my seat and pull my hat down so he doesn't see me. Cami's on her cell phone, distracted, and she glances up at me, squinting. Then she gives J-Dog a quick peck on the cheek and waves good-bye. He doesn't look very satisfied with that, but he turns and walks back into the school. Basketball practice, probably.

Cami hops up the bus steps and sees me, and then she talks on the phone a second more and hangs up. She flops in the seat and says to me, really loud, "Will you please start answering your stupid phone? Your mother called my mother and my mother called me to see if I knew where you were. Somebody marked you down as an unexcused absence from school today and the office called home to find out where you were. Your parents are freaked."

"Shit," I say. They know. Of course they know. The

school would call them. I should have known that. It's been a while since I've had to cut school, and Ellen never really cared.

"What?" Cami's voice is sharp. She folds a piece of gum into her mouth and chews, hard.

"Did you tell your mother I was on the bus?"

"Yeah."

"Okay," I say, thinking fast. "Yeah, that's good."

"Why?"

"I cut school," I say. "I'm not going back. I'm quitting."

"Oh, great." Cami sinks back in the seat. "Ethan, why?"

"I'm sixteen, I can quit if I want."

"Are you sure about that? I bet you have to have your parents' permission."

I stare at her. "How would you know?" But I'm scared she's right.

She just sighs and pulls out her iPod and I feel like a loser. But I'm still not going back there.

We pick up the middle school kids and Blake has his phone out. He gives me a huge smirk when he says, "Bye, Dad," and I know he knows I'm busted. I scrunch down in the seat and just try to breathe all the way home. Try to pretend I'm cool about all of this.

But I am so not.

• • •

I go inside, into the kitchen, and Gracie's eyes are huge, like she's trying to warn me. Blake shoves past and goes to his room. Mama comes around the corner, sees me, and stops. She looks so disappointed.

"Mama," I say. "Can we please talk about this?"

"You had me worried sick. Where were you all day?"

"Just wandering around. I'm sorry. I couldn't do it—"

"Ethan, I want you to promise me you'll go to your classes tomorrow."

"But I have some ideas."

"Like what?" She doesn't look very open to them.

"Like, you could homeschool me. Or maybe I could get a tutor."

She shakes her head and sighs. "I'm not cut out for homeschooling, and we just can't afford a tutor right now."

"I could get a job. I could help pay." I plead with my eyes.

"No. You need to focus on studying and catching up in school. Believe me, Ethan, I've tried convincing your father, okay? It's not going to happen."

"Then I'll quit school."

"You can't," Mama says. "Besides, you're smart. You're just overreacting to one event that everyone's forgotten about already. And you don't even know yet if you'll be in freshman classes. Just take a deep breath and handle it, Ethan! You know you can do it."

I stare at her. Not really sure what to say.

She puts her hand on my shoulder. "Honey, sometimes you just have to suck it up, like everyone else has to." And then she walks past me into the kitchen and starts pulling stuff out of the fridge for dinner.

I look at Gracie and she just shrugs at me. "Suck it up," she says.

# CHAPTER 30

I'm hiding in the basement when Dad gets home,
but he doesn't come after me. We don't discuss my skip
day at dinner, either, and I'm thinking maybe Mama took
care of things. I'm kind of thrilled about that, but it's
freaking me out a little wondering if Dad's going to spring
something on me. The yelling is really getting old, and
I think I'm going to have to try to follow the rules for a
while, just to keep the peace. I can't keep disappointing
Mama when she's sticking her neck out for me. I pick out
some more picture books from a box and start reading, just
to get something calm going in my brain. This angsty crap
is making my chest all weird and congested.

Blake has another assignment for his science class
and he makes an exaggerated effort checking my earlobes

and marking everybody on the chart as either attached or detached. I kind of remember this stuff from middle school and it was sort of interesting. Maybe school won't be so bad after all. I wonder if I really was making too big a deal out of it.

After dinner, Dad and I work on my new bedroom some more. We get the frame totally done and hang the drywall and mud it, which is cool, because he just teaches me how to do stuff and doesn't yell. And all he says about today is, "Let's start fresh tomorrow with school, okay?" And I'm like, "Yeah," and I give a big sigh of relief. I'm glad, really. I am. And I'm going to give it a try. Just suck it up.

I bet Cami will like that.

After Dad goes to bed, I start going through the photos, pulling out all the ones I like. I think I'm going to make a collage for my bedroom. I lay out all the photos on the pool table and arrange them the way I want them, like they tell a story. And I see how happy we were, Mama and Dad and Blake and me, and I get this lump in my throat. Because I want that.

Ellen didn't take many pictures. She'd get one of those disposable cameras now and then, but lots of times it would just sit there for a year or two because we didn't have the money to go get the film developed. I wonder if she's gotten them developed now, or if she just threw them all away. Like she threw me away.

I work until I can't keep my eyes open anymore.

Morning comes too soon.


Cami looks glad to see me at the bus stop.

"Well?" she demands.

"Quitting is for losers." Just saying the words makes my gut hurt.

"You'd better not wander off again like yesterday."

I glance sidelong at her. "Maybe you should hang on to me, then. So I get inside all right."

She blushes and lowers those long lashes. "Don't be dumb."

"I'm not dumb. I'm desperate."

She laughs, like she thinks I'm joking. I like that. It makes me think that maybe I am, too. Like maybe I really can handle it.


I make it through. And it's nowhere near as bad as I thought.

A few people ask me if I'm okay, and I search their faces, suspicious. Are they mocking me? But they seem sincere. At lunch, J-Dog apologizes and I let him. But I sit by myself. I can't deal with him yet. Maybe not ever, who knows? All I know is that this little town of Belleville is full of some pretty decent people. Nothing like I've ever seen before.

. . .

After school I invite Cami to come over and see the prog-
ress of my new bedroom. She spends a long time looking at
all the pictures I laid out on the pool table. Remembering
things. She's in a few of them. At least I think it's her. We
lean over and look together.

"That's you, isn't it?" I ask, pointing to one where I
stand at the dining table working the sno-cone machine.
Blake's just a toddler, and a girl holds a cup, catching the
shaved ice.

She smiles, laughs a little. "Yeah, I remember that!"
And then she looks at me like she said something insensi-
tive. "Sorry . . . Is any of it coming back?"

I ponder that question for a minute. "Sometimes
I think it is." I glance over at the orange racetrack. "It
all feels sort of familiar, but nothing really stands out.
Familiar, like comfortable, you know? Like it feels right,
and I belong here. Most of the time, anyway." I frown.

"You and Blake still fighting?"

"He's not talking to me." I look at the photos where
we are playing together. Where in a family picture, I rest
my hand on his shoulder like I'm protecting him. "I don't
know what to do. He's being such a jerk."

Cami puts a comforting arm around my waist, and
I can feel the side of her boob against my arm. Jesus,
doesn't she know what she's doing? I want her so bad.

But I have to get away or I'll fuck it all up again. I can't do that.

"Why don't you ever do anything with J-Dog?" I ask, standing up straight and turning to face her. "Do you ever go out? I never see you together outside of school."

"Oh," she says. "Yeah, it's basketball season, so . . ." She shrugs like she doesn't care, but her eyes give her away.

"So after basketball season, you'll go out more?"

"Well." She laughs lightly. "Then baseball starts."

"Summer?"

"Golf. His dad's a pro. Jason caddies at the club. And then there are the guys, his friends."

I just look at her. And I feel really bad. I do. Because even though I want her so bad my balls are turning blue, I realize, in this moment, that she's my friend. She's like my first real friend since I got my life back. "I'm sorry," I say. And I really mean it.

"S'okay." She laughs a little, and it sounds hollow. "Sometimes I'm not sure why I keep waiting around for him to be done with everything else."

I nod, and it's a soft moment, all quiet and contemplative. "You know where to find me if you get lonely." And I feel half desperate for saying it and half like I'm actually figuring out how to be a good person, all at once.

"I know," she says. She leans in for a hug, and I can feel her warm sigh down my shirt collar.

# CHAPTER 31

Thursday comes, and after school, we all pile into the car to drop off Gracie at Grandpa and Grandma's while the rest of us go to see Dr. Frost. "She's hot," I say to Blake as we settle into the backseat. He doesn't respond, but I see him smirk a little.

Dr. Frost asks to see Blake and Dad first, since she hasn't met them. She thinks that will help put us all on a fair playing field. So Mama and I sit in the waiting room, paging through magazines. Not talking. Just waiting. I look up at the ceiling fan, which is going slowly, and I picture a helicopter crashing down into the room.

That would get me out of this.

Finally, Dr. Frost comes to get us.

I flash Blake a look when I walk in, as if to say, *Didn't I tell you she was hot?* but his arms are crossed over his chest and he's stone-faced, staring at the carpet. Dad sits next to him and isn't smiling.

It feels a little weird. I glance at Mama, giving Dad a puzzled look. He frowns. We sit down on the sofa, facing Blake and Dad, and Dr. Frost sits in her chair.

"First, I already said this to Blake and Paul," Dr. Frost says, "but I wanted to say it again. I think it's terrific that you all are here and trying to work out some of these issues. You have a unique situation that comes with a unique set of problems, and this is new for all of you. So we'll work through this together the best that we can, all right?"

I nod and picture the happy family in my head, the one I want to be a part of. Something good warms up my insides when Dr. Frost talks like this, and I feel like I can do whatever it takes to have that.

"Great," Dr. Frost says. She looks at a notepad in her lap. "First, Ethan, I know this is hard, but I'd like for you to recount some of what you told me about your years with Eleanor, so that Blake and your dad can hear them firsthand."

I take a deep breath. I wasn't expecting to have to relive the last session. Mama grabs my hand and squeezes it, but I pull away—it's distracting.

And I do it for Dr. Frost. I tell it all again. But I don't look at Blake. I don't want to see how he reacts. I pretend

I'm talking just to Dr. Frost, and I actually get through it without going into hysterics, which is a total relief.

"Thank you," she says. "Now, Blake, your turn. Why don't you say what's on your mind, like you did earlier, before your mom and brother came in."

My stomach flutters.

Blake shifts in his chair.

"Blake?"

He shakes his head. "I changed my mind," he says. "I don't have to say it. I'm not going to. This is stupid."

I look quickly from Dr. Frost to Dad to Blake, and then I glance at Mama, who is trying to act calm, but I can see her gripping the sofa arm. Her fingernails are white.

Dr. Frost addresses Blake. "No, you don't have to say it. I think it would be a good idea if you did, though."

He shakes his head. "No. I really don't think so." He gets up. "I'm going to the waiting room." And then he walks out and shuts the door, hard, behind him. Dad gets up and goes after him.

Mama and I watch him go. And I can't help it. I get a lump in my throat.

"Dr. Frost," Mama says, "is Blake . . . can you tell us what . . . ?"

She shakes her head. "No, I'm sorry, I can't. But I'm sure you can tell he's dealing with some anger issues. He just needs to work through them."

I look at my knees and think about our messed-up family. And really, for the first time, I don't think it's me that's so messed up.

That night, Dad and I work on my bedroom again, and it's almost done. The weekend should do it, he says. We don't talk about the session, but Dad gives me a hug before he turns in, which is different. And good, I think.

I open up the vents, and as I drift off to sleep, I hear the soft sounds of Mama and Dad talking in their bedroom upstairs. The ceiling creaks above me as I imagine them walking around the bedroom, getting ready for bed.

I am almost asleep when I think I hear Dad say, "Blake doesn't believe it's really him."

# CHAPTER 32

My eyes spring open and my stomach muscles seize up.

"What?" Mama says, incredulous.

"He says he doesn't understand how anybody can just forget the first seven years of his life. He listed about fifteen things he remembered from when he was seven or younger before Dr. Frost cut him off."

Mama's voice gets louder. "Did she explain that it's normal? Did she tell Blake that it's common for abducted children to be so traumatized that they forget where they came from? That they often become attached to their abductors as if they are parents?" Mama's fuming, rattling off her clinical facts like she memorized the textbook, and she's loud enough that I wonder if Blake can hear her too, from his bedroom, if he's still awake.

"Shh," Dad says. His tone rumbles above me but I can't make out what he's saying, except for occasional phrases: ". . . talk about it without judging him," and ". . . I don't know how long it'll take . . ."

I can't breathe. How could Blake say such a thing about me? He thinks I'm a fake? Why is he doing this? He has no idea how awful it feels not to remember him. To hardly remember anything. To think it'll all come back to me, but it just doesn't, and it makes me feel so lost.

The usual massive panic crashes into me. I bury my face in my pillow to shield the noise as my body goes out of control and shudders in pathetic, hysterical laughter.

# CHAPTER 33

At breakfast, I can't even look at Blake. It doesn't seem to bother him—he's been ignoring me for days already. Now the animosity is completely mutual. I feel like somebody beat me up. I can't believe it. I'm grateful for Mama, who gives me an extra-long hug before I head out the door today to the bus stop.

There's a game tonight. Cami says she's going, of course. And of course, I am not.

On the bus, Cami's talking about some English paper she's writing, and then she pauses midsentence like she's just seeing my face for the first time. "What's wrong?"

I look at her, and hell if I don't almost start bawling. God, she's just so sweet to even notice. I smile instead and get a grip. "Nothing," I say. I don't want to risk any chance of Blake overhearing. I don't even think I can say the words out loud, they sound so bad.

"No," she says. "Something's wrong. You look terrible. Are you sick?"

I shake my head. "Not physically."

Cami rolls her eyes. "Look, don't play this game. Just tell me."

"I can't talk about it now," I say. "Too many people around, okay?"

"Oh," she says. "Okay. This weekend sometime?"

I smile. "Yes."

She slips her hand in mine and squeezes, and then she lets go. "I'll text you."

J-Dog stops by my table at lunch and harasses me about going to the game tonight, but I just give him a look and he backs off. "Sorry, man. It's not like it's going to happen again, you know."

It's not funny. I don't know if it ever will be.

At the end of the day, I find out that I tested out of all freshman classes. I've got to take geometry with the sophomores, but that's not nearly as bad as algebra with the freshmen. Same with English and history, but I can take summer classes to catch up to the other juniors if I want. At this point, anything that keeps me away from Blake is a good thing, even summer school. I picture him introducing me to strangers as his fake brother, or announcing it at a basketball game or something. Which is stupid for me to worry about, but my gut seizes up just thinking about more Blake drama—it's like a reflex.

I wonder how long our feud is going to last?

I walk Cami home, and we're just talking, but I know she's got to get ready for the game. "If you're bored after," I say, "you can just come around back to the lower-level slider door. I'll see you, or hear you if you tap the glass. You know, if the game is done early and you don't have other plans."

"Or tomorrow," she says. She looks guilty, like she doesn't want to tell me she's finally going out with her boyfriend for once after the game. It's kind of sweet, really.

"Tomorrow's fine, too. You'll text me," I say, remembering. "Absolutely. Have fun tonight."

She gives me this deep-eyed look. "I wish you would come."

I look at the driveway. "Can't. Gotta finish my bedroom. Almost there—I want to paint in the morning and move my stuff in. I'm tired of sleeping on the floor."

"Why haven't you brought your bed downstairs already?"

"Just to piss off Blake after he threw all my shit out into the hallway. Keeping him inconvenienced for as long as possible."

She laughs. "Sounds like he deserves it. What's up, anyway?"

I study her face. "You can't tell anybody. I'm not supposed to know."

She nods emphatically. "Promise."

"Blake thinks . . ." Ugh, I can't say it. I take a breath.

"What?"

"He doesn't think I'm really his brother. He doesn't think I'm Ethan."

Cami stares. "Are you kidding me? What the hell is wrong with him?"

"He's having a tough time," I say, and for a second, I almost feel bad for him.

"I had no idea," Cami says. "I just thought he was jealous."

"Yeah, there's that, too," I say.

"You *have* been getting a lot of attention lately, but still."

"I know, right?"

She shakes her head, the little balls at the top of her wool hat jiggling. "I'm sorry, Eth. That must feel like total crap. What did your parents say?"

"They don't know I know. I heard them talking after we went to the shrink yesterday."

She gives me a quizzical look.

"Family shrink. To help us all deal with everything."

"It's good you're going. Seems like you're doing better now that you're back in school, right?"

I grin. "It was kind of a rough start. Getting smoother."

"So smooth that you want to go to the game? Sit with me?" She bats her eyelashes.

My jaw drops. "You are evil," I say. "Flirting behind your boyfriend's back."

She tilts her head and smiles. "Is that what I'm doing?"

"Evil. I've got to go. Work on my room. Yeah." I take a few steps backward, just getting one more look at her, and then I turn and fly down the street to my house.

When I get home, I find out that Dad took a half day and has all the sanding done and the walls primed for paint, which is extremely awesome. I think they are feeling pretty bad. Mama didn't even yell at me for not calling after being five minutes late getting home.

I let Gracie help me paint while Dad gets the hinges on the doorframe. I actually know how to do this task. Ellen and I painted one of the crappy apartments we lived in. The landlord got some light pink paint really cheap and said if we painted, we could move in right away and he'd take some money off the rent. So we did it. Here, it's basic tan, no frills, no fancy colors. Gracie gets her footie pajamas on and then stays up late "helping," and Mama brings us pizza so we can keep working.

By eleven, the paint is drying, the drop cloths are picked up, the floor is clean, the baseboards are up, and the nail holes are puttied. Gracie's asleep on my quilt over by the pool table, and I have a bedroom. It's huge and I love it. I grin at Dad and he claps me on the back. "Thanks, Dad," I say. "This is awesome."

He smiles. "We're getting there."

As Dad puts paint supplies away and takes care of the brushes, I pick up Gracie to take her to her bedroom. She's a little lump in my arms, sucking her thumb even though she's not supposed to anymore. It's cute. She wraps her other arm around my neck, her head on my shoulder. Never waking up.

Mama's asleep on the couch, a book on her chest and the TV on low. Blake's door is cracked open and his light is on, and I'm tempted to take the bed apart tonight and set it up in my room, but I know Dad's tired and so am I. One more night on the floor won't kill me. I walk into Gracie's dark room and lay her down, tucking her in under the blankets. She's zonked. It makes me happy, you know? To see a little kid all asleep like that, all peaceful, sucking her thumb, her hair a big frizz-mop. . . . It's so calming. I look at her for another minute, feeling all Zen and smiling, and then a shadow hits the doorway.

I look up and it's Blake, glaring at me, shattering the peace with the look on his face.

"You stay away from her," he whispers.

# CHAPTER 34

"Fuck off." I leave Gracie's room, closing the door, and Blake is already down the hallway ahead of me, disappearing into his room. I hesitate at his door, and then realize how not worth it that is. At eleven p.m., with Mama asleep and Dad having spent so much time helping me with my room, I figure avoiding controversy is best.

When I wake up Saturday morning, I look out the slider door and see the sun for the first time since I've been here, I think. Above me, I hear the thunder of little feet, and it sounds like there's a small herd of antelope up there. Either that or Gracie's dancing to Saturday-morning TV shows. I drag my butt to the shower and get ready to move into my room.

By the time I'm dressed, Dad and Blake are coming down the stairs with my bed. Blake must really want all traces of me out of his room if he's willing to help, and I grin to myself. I pretend to be busy in the bathroom and let them haul it all down—my muscles are sore from painting.

When I emerge, I can hear Dad putting the bed frame together, and Blake's standing over by the pool table, looking at my collage of photos. I feel a sudden surge of protectiveness and I don't want Blake touching them. I know it's weird, but I don't want his angry vibes around my stuff. Even though technically he's in the pictures too, so I guess they aren't mine, but still. I need them more than he does.

Blake looks up and narrows his eyes when he sees me. "What's this, your shrine to yourself?"

"No," I say.

"Then what?"

"They're just pictures. I like looking at them. Why do you care?"

Blake looks closer at them. "Do you remember any of these? I do." It's a challenge.

My stomach hurts. "I remember the sno-cone machine. You drank the syrup straight from the little bottles." It's a terrible lie, I know, but I just need him to chill. I need him to chill, and I need to get as much distance between us as possible.

He looks skeptical. "I did not."

"You did. You were really little, so maybe you don't remember." Ha.

"All right, then, what else?"

I'm tempted to make up more, but I have a feeling nothing will satisfy him. Besides, I have nothing to prove. "What's your problem, anyway?"

"You," he says in a low voice. "There's something about you that's not quite right. Something sneaky." He pauses, measuring me with his eyes, a little nervous, even. And then he says it. "You're not Ethan."

Fuck. I can't believe how much the accusation hurts, even though I knew it was coming. I can't even argue against it because it doesn't make any sense. "Blake," I say in an even voice, "you were four. You're not going to remember it the way it really was." I can feel my face getting red, and I fight off the anger. "Whether you like it or not, I'm Ethan De Wilde. Brother to the biggest asshole on the planet." I turn, walk to my room, and close the door quietly, although I want to slam it.

Dad looks up from his spot on the floor, where he's fighting with a wrench. "Almost done," he says, grunting. "Then we can get your mattress on and get your dresser and desk down here."

I smile as brightly as I can manage, but I'm still pissed off. To tell the truth, I feel like shit. Dad doesn't notice.

He turns his attention back to the bed again. I sit down on the floor near him and pull my knees up. "Dad?" My throat starts to ache.

He stops and looks up. "Yes?"

My face twists and I choke the words out. "I know what's up with Blake. He just said it to my face."

Dad frowns, concerned, and then his eyes soften and he sets the wrench down. He shuffles on his knees over to where I'm sitting and looks me in the eye. He shakes his head a little, sighs deeply, and puts his arm around my shoulders. "Oh, buddy," he says. "I am so sorry."

And then I lose it. Dad comes closer and we're hugging awkwardly on the floor, and I'm cough-sobbing stupidly into his shoulder, and he's patting my back. And even though I think he wants to try to give excuses for Blake and his issues, he doesn't. He just tries to comfort me in his own awkward way. That's about the coolest thing he could do.

I'm stretched out on my bed, sun streaming in through my window, trying to enjoy my privacy and trying not to think about what a prick Blake is, when I hear a knock on glass. I hop out of my room and there's Cami, standing at the walk-out slider door, holding a sled. Her face is glowing and she's hatless, her coat open at the neck. She's like a model for a snow commercial or something.

"Come out!" she shouts through the glass.

I unlock the door and open it. "Hey!"

"It's warm today—almost above freezing! Let's go sledding over at the big hill." Her eyes shine, and as much as I hate the cold, I can't say no.

"Do you have a sled for me?"

"Don't you have one?"

"I have no idea—I'll ask." I still feel like such a visitor here sometimes. "Meet you in the driveway."

I take the stairs two at a time and find Mama at the table paying bills and Gracie flopped back dramatically in her chair, probably whining about something.

"Do we have sleds, Mama?" I ask.

She doesn't look up. "Don't you have homework?"

"I can do it tonight or tomorrow. Can I go sledding with Cami? It's nice out for once."

"Fine," she says, distracted.

"I want to go!" Gracie shouts. "Please please please, Efan."

I scowl. "No. You're too little."

Mama looks up. "Oh, that would be a big help if you'd take her. I'm doing taxes." She flips through her checkbook and writes something down. "Just make sure you stay with her at all times. Gracie, no wandering off, you promise?"

I look at Gracie. She's grinning.

"All right," I say, relenting, but I'm thinking there goes my chance at having some time alone with Cami. "Do we have a sled, Macie?"

Gracie giggles. "It's Gracie!"

"Okay, Lacie."

"No no, it's Facie!"

"Whoever you are, get your coat on and let's go."

Gracie marches to get her junk on, and I go dig around in the garage with Cami and find sleds.

"Sorry, I got suckered into babysitting."

She grins. "Ah, well. Gracie's not too bad for a little kid. Could be worse."

"Could be Blake," I mutter.

Cami laughs. "Has he gotten over his paranoia yet?"

"No. It's getting worse."

She shakes her head. "Poor guy."

"Who, me?" I ask.

"No, him. He can't seem to find the right way to get people to like him. Plus, being thirteen sucks."

"True." I think about when I was thirteen. It was the first time Ellen left me alone for more than a few days. Thirteen was also the first time I stole a wallet and ate out of the garbage. And then there was Bree Ann. I suck in a sharp breath and let it out to clear my mind. I don't want to think about them now.

Gracie comes out in her snowsuit and stiffly walks over to us. We grab the sleds and Cami leads the way through the backyards. I drag Gracie along by the hand. Apparently there's a big snow hill at the elementary school nearby.

Confession: I've never been sledding. Not that I remember, anyway.

It's a freaking big hill. And we aren't the only ones to think of doing this today. The place is overrun by little kids.

I hop on one sled and situate Gracie in front of me.

"Ready, guys?" Cami asks.

"Ready," Gracie and I say. Cami pushes on my back and gets us going, and then we're flying down the hill. The wind rushes through my hair and past my ears, and I grip the edge of the sled with one hand, hanging on tightly to Gracie with the other, wondering a little too late how to steer. At the bottom, we hit a snowdrift and for a moment we're airborne before we land and fall off. Gracie's laughing and has snow all on her face, and my butt hurts.

"Now what?" I ask her.

"Now we climb back up and do it again."

I flop back in the snow and look at the sky. "Climb all the way back up?"

"Yeah! It's easy."

"Maybe for a little kid."

She laughs again and flops down on my chest. I pick her up and hold her up above me, then set her down on her feet. "Come on," I say, reaching out my hand. "Pull me up."

She tugs my arm like she's really trying. I roll to my side and get to my feet. We drag the sled up the hill.

Cami's nowhere to be seen—I can only guess that she went down a different way.

And then I see her over to one side. Talking to Blake. Blake gestures with his hands like he's agitated. I squint to get a better look. Cami points in our general direction, and Blake looks around, but he doesn't see us. I glance down at Gracie, who's sitting patiently on the sled again, ready to go. I hop on the sled and we scoot forward until gravity helps out, and then we're flying once more. We almost get sideswiped, but I'm figuring out how to steer a little, and magically we avoid a total collision.

Back up the hill, and Blake finally sees us and comes stomping through the snow. Cami shrugs helplessly at me.

"Uh-oh," I mutter. I don't have a good feeling about this.

Blake looks furious. "What are you doing?"

"We're sledding. Obviously."

He glances at Gracie, sitting again in the sled, waiting. "I was going to take her sledding."

"Well, we're already here. So."

"So, leave."

"No," I say through my teeth. "You leave."

"Forget it." And then he shoves me.

Fuck.

Why'd he have to go and shove me?

# CHAPTER 35

I pound him. I do. With a rush of anger I shove him back, and when he falls, I jump on him, and then before I can even believe I'm doing it, I'm pounding him. His face, his chest, his stomach . . . everything. It's like I'm outside my body, watching myself, completely out of control.

Granted, with me wearing gloves, and him wearing a coat, the damage could have been worse. And if Cami hadn't been there to scream some sense into me and pull me back, it could have been a lot worse. But God. Why does he keep doing things like this? What the hell is wrong with him?

So there he is, his nose bleeding and his lip swelling up, the snow all on one side of him red . . . it reminds me of a cherry sno-cone. And for about ten seconds, it feels good that he's lying there sniveling, because he fucking deserves it.

But I don't know what will happen now.

And there's Gracie, bawling. A crowd gathers around to see what happened.

I'm such a fucking loser.

I get down on my knees in the snow next to Blake. And I offer him my hand. "Come on, man. Get up."

"Go to hell," he says.

"Look, I'm sorry I hit you, but you need to stop starting this shit. Let's get you home. Here, put a snowball on your lip. Come on. Gracie's crying. Everybody's looking."

"Good. Let 'em look. It's good to have witnesses." He narrows his eyes and shoves himself up on his elbows, ignoring my outstretched arm. He rolls to his side and pushes to his feet, and then spits on the ground. "Come on, Gracie," he says, leaning down and grabbing the sled's rope. "Mama won't want you anywhere near him after she hears about this."

My gut twists at the satisfaction in his voice, and suddenly I realize what the bastard is doing. "You planned this?" I ask, incredulous.

Cami's eyes go wide and her lips part. She turns to look at me.

Blake doesn't answer. He pulls Gracie in the sled

toward home, and the crowd of onlookers breaks up when there's nothing more to see.

After a minute, I grab the other sled. "Can you come home with me?" I ask. "I might need a witness."

"Sure," Cami says. "I just can't believe this. You really think he did it on purpose?"

I nod. I'm sure he did. We hurry to catch up so Blake doesn't have much time to corrupt Mama and Dad before I'm there to defend myself. But I know I'm in for it. Big-time.

"Just stay calm," Cami says. "He's trying to get you to do something, and he'll keep trying. If you stay calm and don't let him get his satisfaction that way, you win."

"I have no chance at winning here. Did you see what I did to his face?"

"Yeah, I know," she says. She runs her hand through her hair and looks at me, worried. "But don't make it worse."

"Yeah," I say. "Okay."

"I mean it. Stay calm. Be the rational one. You'll look better."

I know she's right. I suck in a breath and let it out slowly to keep the panic buried as we reach the driveway right behind Blake and Gracie. Gracie hops off the sled and runs to the door. She looks back at me like she's scared of me, and that pretty much just makes me want to shoot myself in the head.

"You're so dead," Blake says to me as he goes inside.

I turn away, and now I don't want to go in at all. I'm scared. I don't want to hear it—Mama all upset about Blake's face, Dad furious at me, all the yelling. "I can't go in there," I say.

"Let's just sit out here on the step. It's nice out."

But I'm not thinking, not feeling the temperature, not feeling anything. "I think maybe I should go." I sit down on the step and whip off my bloody gloves. Pinch the bridge of my nose, where a headache is starting.

"Where?"

"Away. Maybe back to the south. To find Ellen . . . nor." I can feel Cami staring at me, but I can't look at her. I don't want to think about leaving her behind. Not now, when I'm just getting her to like me, maybe. A little. But I can't keep living like this, I really can't. Constant tension in the house . . . and Blake . . .

And then I think about Gracie and how she looked at me. Like I betrayed her. I don't know if I can look her in the eye again. Such a little sweet kid—she doesn't need to grow up and see this kind of crap.

"Ethan," Cami says softly. Finally. "Eleanor's not the right answer. Don't you think that would be even harder to go back to? Plus, isn't she, like, wanted by the police?"

I squinch my eyes shut and I don't want to think about that. I had good times with Ellen. She really liked me, too. I know she did. She chose me, for fuck's sake. Out of all the kids in the world, Ellen chose me. And she hired those guys, or whatever, to kidnap me. Me, not Blake. Not Cami. Not some other kid down this street, or any street in Belleville or St. Paul or New York or Hollywood. She chose *me*. She wanted me. Somebody fucking wanted me.

How could she stop wanting me?

I know something must have happened to her for her to not come back for me in Nebraska. Because she always came back. Always. And now I wonder if I've made a terrible mistake. I abandoned her by not going out to find her. What if she needed me and came back to the youth home, and I wasn't there? What if she did actually see news of my return to my real family, and she's so sad now?

The sickness is roiling inside of me—the panic and the laughter. That's what it is, I think. It's a sickness. I didn't have it when I was a little kid, I know that by the look of horror on Mama's face when she watched me spin out of control at Dr. Frost's. And I feel it there now, heavy, like I swallowed a boot—yeah, like I swallowed a goddamn boot and it's trying to hike its way up my ribs, trying to get out. And I don't want to let it, because Cami's here and she'll think I'm a total freak if it happens, but it's so strong I don't think I can stop it. I don't have any control. I push my head between my knees and try to suck in some air.

"Ethan, are you okay?"

I nod and flash her the okay sign, but she still looks worried. I want to get away from her so she doesn't see it. I want to run, but I know what'll happen. Same thing that happened at the basketball game. I need every ounce of air I can get so I don't pass out and fall down. How would that look, huh? Pretty fucking worse than if I sit here and let the sickness run its course.

And it does.

It sounds like I'm dry heaving, but then the hysterical laughter spews out.

Cami, fidgeting and anxious, stands up. "Ethan, do you need help? I'll get your mom!"

I grab her wrist. Shake my head and cover my face, so she doesn't see it all ugly and distorted. I hold her arm and she sits down next to me, looking helpless, and then she puts her arm around my shoulders and holds on. I hold up my forefinger to let her know I'm almost through it. But I know, once I'm through, Cami's not going to want to be anywhere near a freak like me.

I can't help it now, though. I can't hide it. I need her.

When I can finally speak, all I can say between gasps is, "I'm sorry. I'm really not as fucked-up as I seem."

"Man." Cami shakes her head. "What was that all about?" She's not leaving.

"It's just a problem I have. Some sort of nervous reaction to stress after all the crap I've been through, I guess. Doctor says I'll probably grow out of it."

"Uh, it might help if you could cut down on the drama," she says.

"You think?"

She grins. God, I love her. I do.

We sit there together, growing cold on the steps, waiting.

# CHAPTER 36

And it's not good. It's really not. It goes something like this.

Dad: You're grounded for life. I have a thousand chores for you to do, including kissing Blake's ass. No friends over. Cami, go home forever.

Me: But, Dad, he started it.

Dad: Family meeting tonight after everybody calms down. For now, you are dead to me.

At least that's how it feels. I lie on my bed and stare at the ceiling. I have never been grounded before. Ellen always just let me do whatever, and I didn't get into much trouble. Here, with all these rules . . . it's like a trap I can't stay away from. After a while I pick up my pile of clothes. They're still in a tangled mess on the floor where I put them after Blake tossed my stuff out of his room. I sort through them, fold them, and put them all away.

After that, I drag all the boxes marked ETHAN into my room and stack them in the corner where they'll be safe. And then I go over to the pool table to gather up the collage of photographs.

But it looks like a tornado went through it. The photos are flipped over and scattered around like somebody picked them all up and threw them into the air, letting them stay wherever they fell. And I'm beyond pissed off.

Several of them are missing. And a couple of them are ripped.

And it's not okay. It really isn't. My breathing gets all shallow and scratchy and I don't know what to do—I just circle the pool table, not knowing where to start, how to fix it. Finally I snatch up the remaining photos and bring them into my room, wishing I could get a lock for my door. I sit down on the floor and spread them out, gently, trying to breath normally. And as I attempt to re-create the collage exactly as before, I stare at the empty spots, trying to remember which ones are no longer there. It's like trying to plug in the broken pieces of my life. I can't remember what's missing.

I text Cami. *Guess what? Blake wrecked my photos.*

She replies instantly. *Jerk. Wait, you still have phone privs?*

*Yeah. They wouldn't take that away. They're obsessed w/ keeping track of me.*

*I noticed. But can you blame them?*

I think about that. *No, I guess not.*

*At least we can still talk this way.*

I smile and type. *Yeah. Family meeting tonight. Should be interesting. Will let you know!*

*I'll be waiting.*

I bite my lip. *No date tonight? It's Sat. No games or practice.*

She doesn't answer for a while. And then all she says is, *Nope, I'm busy with some other projects at home tonight.*

*Like?*

*Like . . . making sure you live through the family meeting. *grin**

She makes me calm. She does. I don't know how she does it. *Sneak over tonight if you dare. Everybody's avoiding me like the plague so it's pretty safe.*

*Maybe. I gotta go now tho, k?*

*Yeah . . . thanks. You made me feel better.*

*Duh.*

I grin and shove my phone into my pocket. And I look at the photographs, laid out like before, but with gaping holes now, and it's killing me trying to remember which ones aren't there. The one with Cami and the sno-cone machine is missing. I know that much.

Maybe once he has Gracie on his side, he'll try to take Cami away too.

# CHAPTER 37

With the blood washed off, Blake's face doesn't look nearly as bad. His swollen lip has gone down a little already and his nose looks normal. He does have a gray shadow under one eye and a red spot on his cheekbone, but they're hardly war wounds. He sits in a chair at the far side of the room. Mama and Dad sit on the couch, Gracie between them. I slip into the remaining chair as the grandfather clock starts chiming six. I look at Gracie, and she looks at me, solemn.

*I'm sorry.* I mouth the words and make a sad face.

She smiles grimly, way beyond her years, and I feel like we're on some dumb TV drama again. I worry that she's here. She shouldn't be here. But I don't know where she'd go. Maybe Mama and Dad think there's still a chance we can have some magical perfect family or something. Maybe by calling it a family meeting, in their minds it means peace, love, and happiness.

Dad lays down the rules. Everybody gets a chance to speak. No raised voices. Calm and civil. Yeah, right.

Mama says, "We've heard Blake's side of the story already. Ethan, let's start with you. Tell us what happened today."

I feel like we're all in kindergarten. "Cami and I decided to go sledding and you asked me if I'd take Gracie, which I did. We walked over to the big hill and Gracie and I went down the hill together a couple times, and we were having a blast, when Blake came storming over. For some stupid reason, after ignoring her for as long as I can remember, Blake is suddenly superprotective of Gracie and he even threatened me last night to stay away—"

"That's because you're a *stranger*!" Blake roars. "You guys, I'm trying to tell you. He's a phony. That's not Ethan!"

Mama raises her arms. "Stop it, Blake." She points to me to continue.

I feel mildly redeemed. "He told me to stay away from Gracie, which is crazy. I think he's just jealous that Gracie and I get along."

"I couldn't care less," Blake says. "I'm just trying to save her life."

"Boys. Calm down," Dad warns.

Gracie looks alarmed and Dad whispers something to her.

"This is not fair," I say, and I struggle to be calm, remembering what Cami said, but my voice pitches higher. "He's scaring her. Will you please tell Gracie that she doesn't have to be scared of me? Sheesh."

"But he's violent!" Blake says. "Look at what he did to me."

I sit up in my chair. "You started it! You start it every time. You throw a punch or shove me and you expect me to walk away? Forget it. I wasn't raised to be a pussy." I turn to Mama. "Maybe you guys need to teach sonny boy here to stop starting shit!"

"Don't use that language in this house," Dad says, and he's looking upset, like he just realized he lost control of this. "It's unacceptable."

"What's unacceptable," I say, "is that you are letting Blake get away with stuff because 'things are tough for him.' Oh, poor Blake. Try trading places with me, Blakey. Try taking your antagonizing act to the streets. You'll see where that gets you." I laugh bitterly. "In the morgue."

"Mama, he just threatened to kill me. He's not safe. And he's not Ethan." Blake has a smug look on his face.

"Blake," Dad says. "That's enough. Both of you."

I think I'd feel more hurt by the accusation if Blake had

any credibility left, but it's clear he doesn't. What hurts, though, is that Mama and Dad aren't making him stop.

Gracie sits quietly on the couch, wide-eyed. I feel bad for her. I do. She's stuck in this mess. I half-smile at her and she half-smiles back. Then it's like Mama realizes Gracie's here and this family meeting isn't what she thought it would be. "Paul," she says, and gives Dad a look. Dad picks Gracie up and takes her to her room, and I'm glad they finally got some sense.

"Blake," Mama says, "Gracie said she saw you shove Ethan before he started punching you. You neglected to tell us that little bit."

"I did not!" Blake says. It's ambiguous as to what he's denying—the shove, or the neglecting to tell—but either way, he looks guilty.

I feel a warm rush of love toward Gracie, stepping up to defend me. I owe her big.

"And Ethan," Mama continues, "as a matter of fact, I *do* expect you to walk away from a shove. You're older, and you need to be the bigger person here."

"But, Mama! He starts it every time! That's not fair—" I start to protest further, but she holds her hand up.

"No," she says. "Shh. Just listen. It's this simple. I don't care how that horrible woman raised you or what you've had to resort to, but when you live here, you're going to follow my rules. Clear?"

My jaw drops as her words cut into me. Did she just insult Ellen and me? I think she really did.

Dad comes back and sits next to Mama.

And Mama stares at me, waiting. "I said, is that clear?"

"Yes, ma'am," I finally say in a cold voice. "But will you please make Blake stop scaring Gracie—"

"Quiet," Mama says. She turns to Blake. "Now, Blake, this nonsense about Ethan not being Ethan has to stop. Really. I know you're hurting, but you need to control your words, especially in front of Gracie. I know it's really hard for you, and that things are different than you expected. But this isn't going to solve anything. It only makes things harder and it's really hurtful, not just to Ethan, but to all of us. So stop. Okay?"

Blake folds his arms over his chest. "I think you should get a DNA test."

I feel my face heat up. "Jeez!" I shout at him. I can't help it. "Can you not shut up?"

Dad sits up like he's ready to grab me if I go after Blake, but I stay in my chair like a good son. Dad gives me a long look, then turns to Blake. "Blake, that's enough," he says with finality. "Done."

Blake shrugs and looks sullen.

It'll take all my strength to keep from killing him with my bare hands.

# CHAPTER 38

It's dark and way after ten when I hear fingernails tapping on glass. I almost fall over myself getting
from my room to the slider door. I let her in and slide the
door closed again, smooth and quiet.

"You made it! You are awesome," I whisper. She brings
crisp air in with her and it wakes me up.

She grins. "How did it go? Awful?"

"Pretty bad."

Cami unzips her coat and slips it off. We sit on the
floor by the slider in the dark, away from any heat vents,
since noise obviously travels both ways. And in case she
has to make a fast getaway. "But it's over. I just hate that
Blake is making Gracie scared of me."

"Do you think Gracie is really scared of you? Or is she scared of the fighting?" she asks.

"I don't know," I say. And I don't. "I wonder if she thinks I could ever possibly hurt her because I hurt Blake?"

"Would you?"

"Of course not. Never." I search Cami's face. "Do you think I would?"

"No," she says. "Not even if you wanted to."

But that's not enough for me. I ask, "Do you think I would ever hurt you?"

Her black eyes are sweet. "No way. Never."

I sit back, relieved. "What did you do tonight?" I ask. I like how this is, sitting here in the dark, whispering. It gives me goose bumps to have her this close, this intimate.

She waves her hand like there was nothing of note, and then she says, "My mom and I do this thing once a month where we make a hundred and fifty sack lunches for the shelter. They hand them out to the shelter patrons so they can have a meal on the road when they go find work and stuff. So, yeah," she says, almost like she's embarrassed to tell me. "Tonight we did that." She laughs. "My fingers still smell like peanut butter."

She breaks my heart, she really does. Does she have any idea how much I counted on shelter sack lunches? They were gold. "Let me smell," I say.

She holds her fingers to my face and I take her hand. It's soft. I close my eyes and breathe in. I can smell the peanut butter, barely. I open my eyes and she's watching me. I hesitate, moisten my lips. Then softly kiss the tip of her forefinger. And she stares at me.

I swallow hard. Hold her fingers to my lips, and she doesn't pull her hand away. I kiss her second fingertip, and then her third. Her pinkie. And then I go back to her forefinger and run my tongue over the tip of her fingernail, my eyes never leaving hers. Her eyelids close halfway, and I circle her fingertip with my tongue and then kiss it again.

She leans in.

I can feel her breath on my lips.

I think I'm going to pass out.

And then she kisses me, so fucking sweet I want to hold her forever.

It lasts ten seconds, maybe more. Feels like more. But then we break the kiss and we both sit back and just breathe and look at each other.

"That was hot," Cami says. "Yikes."

I nod and try to shift without making it obvious that I've got a boner the size of a nun-chuck. "Yikes?" I ask. "That's not the usual reaction, you realize, right?" Tempest never said "yikes." She always said "more." But I don't want to think about Tempest ever again.

She blushes and I can see her sexy bottom lip shining.

"I mean, it was awesome. A little too awesome. I—" I can see the guilt in her eyes.

"Don't," I say quietly. "Just wait one second." I lean in, brush her chin with my fingers, and take her bottom lip in my teeth, running my tongue over it, and I can feel her shiver. I kiss her full on, taste her tongue, and think I'm going to die. My fingers slide through her hair and she slips her arms around my neck, and here we are, crazy, both of us starving for this. And I don't want to think about why I am starving, or why she is; I just want to kiss her, taste her, be with her.

Before she says it. Before she gives me those sad eyes and makes excuses and gets her J-Dog regret all over everything. And when this kiss winds down, I'll walk away and let her be with him, and I'll be okay with just the memory of it. Because it's enough. It has to be enough.

It's not enough.

We're like South America and Africa. Like two continents that exist far away from each other, so totally different from one another, but if you push them together, if you nestle Brazil up into the armpit of Nigeria, it all fits, like they were made for each other. Like they were of the same skin. Like one broke away from the other a long time ago, but now it's back. A puzzle, completed.

I'm back. And I want my other skin.

I've never kissed for love before.

• • •

When it ends, I search her eyes. I don't know if she feels like I feel, or if she's conflicted. I don't blame her for being conflicted about J-Dog. I don't.

As for me, I'd run out in front of a bus if she told me to. I can't hide it. She's got me so caught up in her. I am Nigeria and she's my Brazil, and we exist in this moment, in this quiet, dark little spot by the slider door.

But all I can think of to say, right here, right now, is "Please give me a chance."

Her face is a conflicted story. The wrinkle of her forehead, the line of her eyebrow, the swell of her lips. Her eyes flicker, searching mine.

And then she reaches up, touches my cheek. And says, "Okay."

I stare. I can't help it. "What did you say?"

"I said okay."

I want to shout for joy, but instead I pick up her coat and bury my face in it, trying not to make any noise, a huge grin spreading across my face. And then I grab her and kiss her and we're laughing and shushing each other.

When I can get my breath, I realize what she has to do now. "Oh, shit," I say, my grin fading. "He's going to kill me."

Cami shrugs. "I don't think he'll kill you."

"But . . . are you sure?"

She smiles. "Let's lie low for a while, okay? I'll break up with him tomorrow. I won't say it's because of you.

We'll keep it normal, like we have been. I'm sure he'll pick up another girl to string along and it'll be all good." Her voice is a little bitter. I like that more than I should.

And I feel like a coward, but I like her plan too. I nod.

She sits up and smoothes her hair. "I should get home before my mother freaks. It's late."

We kiss again at the door, and then she slips out into the shadows and through the backyards to her house. I close my eyes and lean against the doorframe for a minute, letting it all sink in. I can't stop grinning. Finally, something is going my way.

I'm starving. I go upstairs for a late-night snack and I'm surprised to see a light still on in the living room. I grab a bran muffin from a basket on the counter and make my way over to the living room to see if it's Mama snoozing on the couch, and then I stop short.

It's Blake. He's studying my second-grade photo on the wall.

I narrow my eyes. "What are you doing?"

Blake wheels around, surprised.

I take a bite of my muffin.

"Nothing," he says. He shoves past me and goes to his room.

But not even Blake can faze me right now. I turn out the light and go back down to my little stress-free cave to dream about my girl.

# CHAPTER 39

Sunday morning Mama drags us all to church, and I'm surprised it's held right at my high school—no church building. There are a few people dressed up, but mostly they're just wearing jeans and sweaters. The music isn't too bad, but I don't sing. Still, I'm surprised at how normal it is and really glad nobody makes me stand up or be healed or come to Jesus or whatever, like they do on TV.

Gracie sticks with Dad. Blake and I keep our distance from each other, and Mama looks like she'll beat the crap out of us if we do anything. I'm not about to cross her on that. My new goal is to get my ass ungrounded so I can spend more time with Cami.

I look around the place and see a lot of people who look familiar, like from school. Cami and her family are on the other side of the auditorium and I swear I start sweating just seeing her. And when church is done and we turn around to go home, I see J-Dog and I get that scary thing in my gut. But he goes the other way and I watch him weave through people toward Cami.

I don't think she's broken up with him yet because he slips his arm around her. My feet cement themselves in place and I can't take my eyes away. He leans down and kisses her and I'm getting sick. But she laughs and pulls away and shoves her purse under her arm, like it's a buffer, and that feels better to me. It's cool, because she doesn't even know I'm here, so I feel good about it. It's like what she said last night actually stayed alive until today— it didn't die after a good night's sleep, like most crazy good things do. I look up at the ceiling and think, *Thank you, God,* even though I'm pretty sure he's not up there hanging around in the high school rafters or on the catwalk.

And when Cami and J-Dog start walking out and talking together, they look serious. Cami spies me and she flashes a big, quick smile of surprise, happy to see me. She nods like we have a plan, and I make a fist and hold it to my chest, like it's her heart next to mine.

God, when did I turn into such a fucking sap?

I catch up to my parents and, big surprise, they didn't even notice I wasn't with them for the past forty-five seconds.

Maybe they think church is safe or something. That's a mistake, if you ask me.

We hang out while Mama talks with some other ladies. Lots of them are so happy to see me and tell me how much they've prayed for me all these years and how they felt when they found out I was home. It's touching, really, because they get all teary about it. I like that. I just hope God doesn't get all the credit for bringing me home, because I sure hitchhiked a hell of a long ways and walked my frozen feet off to get here.

Blake leans up against the wall and doesn't look at anybody, doesn't say anything, and nobody talks to him. And Gracie hops down the middle of the school hallway like the floor has hopscotch painted on it, running into people and being generally adorable. They all love her—everybody knows her name and gives her candy and shit like that. I watch her work the grandpa and grandma types and I gotta give her props. She knows what she's doing.

Every now and then I scan the place for Cami and J-Dog, but I don't see them. My stomach twists a little again, but I'm in control. I think about texting her, but I don't want to get in her face about it. She'll do it when she does it. And I'll wait.

And then it's time to go. We head out to the diner nearby for brunch. I guess it's our family tradition to do that after church. And that's cool. I like it. We are all on our best behavior. Mama and Dad talk about the service and they ask if I liked it.

I shrug. "Sure. It was fine."

Mama looks pleased.

Gracie colors on the kids' menu between bites of her burger, and even Blake passes the pepper when I ask him for it. We talk about plans for the week, and I still don't know half the people they are talking about. Feels like I'm in a play and I don't know all my lines.

I wait for the buzz in my pocket.

At home, everybody disperses. I go down to do my homework and doodle for a while, distracted. And then I go upstairs and wander, trying to find something to do so I don't go crazy. Dad's taking a nap and Mama and Gracie are in the living room playing a board game. Blake is nowhere. In his room as usual, probably.

I hesitate and then sit down on the floor. "Hey," I say. Things are still a little awkward from yesterday. I haven't really talked to either one of them alone since the family meeting. "What are you playing?"

"Chutes and Ladders," Gracie says. "Duh."

I laugh. "Well, I don't know. I've never played it before."

Mama looks at me and gives me this heartbreaking smile. "This was your favorite game."

"I'm sorry I don't remember." I draw my knees up and hug them, rest my chin on them. "What else was my favorite?"

Mama shakes her head. "Just look at Gracie. She's the mirror image of you. She likes practically everything you liked."

Gracie steals a wary glance at me. "Mama, is he the real Efan or the fake Efan?"

"He's the real deal, sweetie. There's no fake Ethan. Blake's just having a tough time."

I smile at Mama. "Thank you," I say.

Gracie looks relieved too. "You're the real deal," she says, like she likes that phrase.

"Yep," I say. "Maybe I even had a lunch box like you. Did I, Mama?"

Mama smiles. "*Star Wars*. It was Dad's old lunch box from when he was a kid, from the first time those movies came out. So yours was a second-generation lunch box, if you can believe it lasted that long. I bet it's still around somewhere, all beat-up."

"What did I keep inside it?" I ask Mama, but I give Gracie a sidelong glance that makes her fume. She knows I'm trying to figure out what's in hers.

"I don't know," Mama says. "Probably your lunch. Or maybe your treasures."

"I want to know what my treasures were so I can know

what Gracie hides in her lunch box," I say, laughing. "I suppose I liked those movies too."

"You were obsessed. You and your Dad watched them over and over."

I ask Gracie, "Are you obsessed with *Star Wars* too?"

"Huh?"

"Do you like to watch the *Star Wars* movies a lot?"

"Nope," she says. "I never even seen 'em."

"Maybe we can watch one together sometime, because I sure don't remember them," I say.

"See, we're the same," she says. I love her logic. And I think maybe that's why I actually like the kid so much. She's about where I was when I left off. It's like I can relive my missing years at her level or something.

We play a few games of Chutes and Ladders. After a while Mama goes to take a nap. Gracie and I hang out having a contest, trying to make the goofiest face. The kid sure likes sticking her fingers in her nose. It's a good distraction.

Blake doesn't come out.

"What do you think Blake does in his room all the time?" I ask Gracie after a while.

"He plays on the 'puter."

"Oh." The computer in Blake's room was supposed to be for both of us to share, but when he threw my stuff out, he didn't hand that over, so basically it's all his. "What does he do on the computer?"

She shrugs. "I don't know. He doesn't let me come in. Only stand in the hallway and peek in."

"Maybe he's a mad scientist creating a robot that will rule the world," I say.

"That's dumb. Play elevator with me."

I groan. I'm tired of playing. She stands on my knees and holds my hands and bounces a little until I bend my knees and she goes up in the air. "What did you do before I was here to play with you?"

She grins and says, "I was waiting for you."

# CHAPTER 40

*It's all good,* Cami texts.

Finally. I almost drop the phone trying to type fast. *Really? He's not going to kill me? Can you come over later?*

*I'll try. I miss you.*

Oh, hell. That kills me, it really does.

I fall asleep with my clothes on, waiting. When I wake up, my alarm clock is blaring. It's morning.

When I see her walking to the bus stop early, I grab my coat and backpack and head out. We're the first ones there.

"Nice plan," I say. "I missed you." We stand with our backs to the house, a noticeable space between us.

"I was hoping you were watching. We're so sneaky."
Cami grins. "Sorry about last night. Too much homework
and I didn't realize how late it was, and then I didn't want
to wake you up."

"Are you okay? I mean, about Jason?" I hate saying
his name.

"Yeah, it's weird. But it's fine." She shrugs. "He didn't
even take it very hard."

"Bastard," I say before I realize I should be glad.

She squints at me and smiles. "You're sweet. I like you.
Wanna make out?"

I laugh. "Right now?"

"I'm kidding. We should still keep it quiet. Give it a
week or so. You think?"

"Yeah," I say, and I'm relieved. I don't want to be the
guy that messed around with J-Dog Roofer's girlfriend . . .
even though I am. That would not work out in my favor.
"Does he know about me?"

"No. I just told him what I'd been thinking for weeks."

"Which is . . . ?"

"That I'm tired of being his girlfriend only when he
runs out of other things to do."

Other students have drifted over and we don't say
much, but when we sit together on the bus as usual, Cami
sits so close to me I can't even concentrate. She just listens
to her playlist, being all sexy, and I look out the window,

thinking about how the last time I rode this bus, I didn't stand a chance.

It's amazing how everything can change just like that.

At school, I know I won't see Cami, because I never do, but I look for her anyway. And, of course, I don't have any trouble finding J-Dog. But we haven't actually talked since his apology, and I think he's figured out that no matter how cool he is, he's never going to get me to go to another basketball game again in my entire life. So at least he's smart enough to give up on me.

I watch him walk around school being all jock and joking around with his friends and flirting with other girls, and he doesn't even look sad. He looks exactly the same. And I think about Cami, how I'd feel if she dumped me, and I can't even imagine it. I definitely wouldn't be walking around like nothing happened.

The best part of the day is when I walk out of school after the bell rings and there's no J-Dog making out with Cami by the bus. She's standing there, though, hair flipped to one side, backpack over one shoulder. Waiting. Waiting for me.

It's a good week. Midterms keep Cami and me both busier than we want to be, and I have extra punishment chores like cleaning out the garage, which has got to be the worst job ever. The garage floor is disgusting. Big stalactites of filthy slush build up behind the car wheels and drop off, getting smashed again when the car goes out—Gracie calls it car poop. I shovel it up and toss it all on the side of the house.

But I also start driver's training and that's probably the most fun I've ever had. I am a natural at it—that's what my instructor says. Finally, I have a talent. Maybe I'll become a race-car driver. That would make my dear, protective Mama happy. I laugh a little just thinking about it.

Blake stays holed up in his room every night working on a school project, or so he claims. I think he's just being emo, but I don't really care as long as he stays away from me and isn't planning to blow up the house or something.

I do my homework at the dining table now. It feels nice to be close to people. I don't know how Blake can stand it, being alone in his room all the time. I like the normal house noises. I like hearing Gracie laugh at cartoons or Dad running the vacuum cleaner or Mama reading aloud something outrageous from the newspaper.

And it finally starts to feel okay that I miss Ellen now and then, but also that I'm done with her. I mean, if I saw her on the street, would I talk to her? Yeah, I would. But now I feel like home is here, not there. That's a first. And it's scary. It is. But it's good. It's so, so good.

On Thursday, Mama downgrades my groundedness from "indefinitely" to "one week," so that means on

Saturday, I'll be free if I can avoid getting into more trouble.

Which is almost impossible because I can hardly stand not seeing Cami. On school nights she can't be out after ten, and here everybody but Gracie is awake until at least that, so it's too risky for her to sneak over. Plus, somebody's bound to see the footprints in the snow if they just think to look. I'm sure Blake would jump at the chance to turn my ass in.

So even though it's a great week, it's horrible, because all I get of Cami is a few minutes at the bus stop and on the bus, where we pretend nothing's going on. And by Friday, I'm dying to touch her and hold her, just be close to her and whisper with her in the dark. Instead, after school we sit in our bedrooms four houses away from each other, texting each other like mad and dreaming about tomorrow.

After dinner Friday, Dad decides it's guys' night out, and he takes Blake and me to a movie. Some lame *Star Wars* look-alike, I guess. Blake doesn't speak to me, but I catch him staring at me throughout the movie. It's really unsettling. It is. It's like he thinks I'm behind a one-way mirror or something and he's watching an interrogation, like a cop. I think he's doing it on purpose to try and wind me up. Get me in trouble again. I just want to punch him.

But I've got only a few hours until I'm free, and there's no way I'm going to screw that up. Besides, I promised

Cami I wouldn't mess this up. I send a text message to her now and then, though Dad's frowning on that tonight.

After the movie, we go for something to eat, and Blake's all embarrassed because what if his friends are here and he's out with his dad rather than the Crips or Bloods or whatever. Jeez, he's so immature. He doesn't have a clue what it's like to never have this chance. To not have a dad to go out with. I wish he'd just grow up. It'd be great if he got to be homeless and abandoned for a while, just to see what it's like.

Anyway, I play the good son and I hope it gets me points. I'm going to want a lot of points saved up just in case. But the weird thing is, Dad is not so bad. He's interesting and has a lot of cool insights about the movie and the graphics and junk like that—stuff you'd never think he'd care or know anything about.

Back at home, Blake slithers to his room. I sit down at the kitchen table with Mama and Dad and we talk about the movie. Mama has to keep shushing Dad and me because Gracie's asleep and we're laughing too loud about the bad special effects. But all the while I'm sort of itching to text with Cami. I finger my phone in my pocket.

Then Blake comes out of his room. He's carrying a red folder. And he's got a creepy look on his face, almost like he's a little bit scared about how evil he really is.

# CHAPTER 41

Blake walks up to the table and our conversation stops.

"Hey, Blake," Mama says cheerily, because we're all pretending we get along today. "Pull up a chair. Did you think the movie was cheesy too?"

Blake doesn't sit down. Instead, he puts the folder on the table and says, "I can prove that he isn't Ethan." His voice cracks when he says my name.

And for a moment, it's completely silent.

I stand up, feeling the blood rushing to my head. "Sorry. I can't deal with this crap anymore." I step aside as calmly as I can and push my chair in, but Blake moves to block me as I round the table.

He stands there inches from me. I can feel the heat

coming off him. He's scared shitless. "No," he says in a surprisingly even voice. "I want to see your face when I prove to my parents that you're a fake."

My jaw aches, but I clench it even harder. Thinking of Cami. Hours away from Saturday. "Mama," I say, not taking my eyes off Blake. "Will you ask Blake to let me through, please?"

"Blake, honestly," Mama says. Her voice is sharp.

"I need him to see this," Blake insists.

"Guys, sit down. Let's work through it," Dad says. When we don't move, he says it louder, more forcefully. "Both of you. Sit down."

I hesitate a minute longer, but the mantra is in my head. Cami. Cami. Cami. I can't allow myself to react. I can't get myself grounded again. If he throws a punch, I won't move. I'll take it and let them deal with him. And so I sit. Numb. The ticking of the kitchen clock sounds like a time bomb. I make my eyes dart around the room in time with it.

Blake sits too. And he looks at Mama and Dad. "I know you don't believe me," he says. "I know you think I'm just angry. And I'm sorry for causing trouble. But you've got to listen to me. Just . . . please. Listen to me for once."

Mama rubs her temples. Dad sits quietly. My chest is tight and I can't take a deep breath. Anticipating rejection is the worst. But all I allow myself to think about is Cami.

Get through this, and I get to see her tomorrow. Fuck it up, and I don't. I focus.

"Go ahead, then," Mama says with an impatient sigh. "Just know that you are on really shaky ground, mister. So watch it."

Blake wets his lips and I can see his fingers shaking. "Okay, so in science, we're doing genetics, right? Dominant and recessive genes. I had to do the eye color thing and the earlobes, remember?"

I wince as pain shoots through me, remembering how bad that made me feel.

"Yes, we remember," Dad says. His face looks tired.

"Well, first there was all the stuff Ethan said about the woman, but I saw two men in the car, and that didn't make sense . . . and him not remembering things—"

"That's perfectly normal," Mama interrupts.

"I know," Blake says quickly, a little too loudly, but he holds his temper in check. "But then I noticed something." He glances at me with such enmity in his eyes, it's stunning.

Blake opens up his folder and pulls out a photograph. It's a slightly blurry, blown-up snapshot—the one of me and him and Cami and the sno-cone machine.

"You stole that from my collection, you little f—" I cut myself off just in time, but neither Mama or Dad notice. They're looking at the photo. I bend forward a little, suck in some air.

"Look at his . . ." Blake's voice cracks again. He clears his throat and points to my head in the photo. "Look at his ear," he says, softer, his voice losing a little of the confidence he had before. His face turns red, and his lips press so tightly together they turn gray.

And I'm sitting here with that boot in my gut. Making its steady climb up my ribs again. Fuck. I try breathing steadily but I'm gulping air.

"What about it?" Mama says.

"He looks different," Blake says. "Do you see it?"

Mama sits back in her chair, exasperated. "Blake, of course he looks different. That's normal. And Ethan looks almost exactly like the age-progression photo that NCMEC created. You look different from then too, because your body and features change a little as you get older."

"Mama," Blake says, and I can tell he knows she's about to blow. "My looks changed, I know. But my earlobes didn't. Earlobes don't change. They are either attached or detached, and they stay that way for life. Ethan's is detached in this picture, see? Now look at him."

Dad leans forward and stares at the photo. He takes it by the corner and pulls it closer so he can see better.

And then he stares at me. At my ears. All the color drains from his face. And his eyes . . . his eyes.

I turn away, but it's too late. His rejection is suffocating, my lungs searing as if I've been underwater too long. I'll never forget that look on his face.

I struggle to my feet as the first wave of hysterics washes over me. I'm falling out of a fifty-story window, I can't breathe, can't do anything but grasp at air and wait for the impact to kill me. I stumble blindly around the table to the basement door and hang on to the handrail in a silent scream as Mama says in a trembling voice like death, "Blake, you have pushed this too far. Go to your room."

# CHAPTER 42

I sit in the dark in my old familiar spot beneath the vent, curled up with a blanket, my teeth chattering. Numb. Mama and Dad arguing. And I can hear Blake up there too. Yelling and throwing crap around in his bedroom, stomping around. And then he's crying, big coughing, angry sobs as Dad tries to talk to him.

"Give me the original photo!" Dad says.

"No. Then I don't have any proof!"

After that, they lower their voices and I can't hear them anymore.

Mama and Dad fight long into the night, and this time, they're not even trying to keep their voices down. I can hear every word.

"It's clearly photoshopped," Mama says, her voice ragged. "And this is a horrible game. It's not funny. I can't believe he would do something so . . . so . . . mean. What kind of boy have we raised? Paul?"

"I don't know," Dad says. "He won't give me the original picture." And that's about all he says. Over and over as Mama rants, he can't answer her and he can't support her. And when she finally winds down, he says wearily, "Maria, sweetheart. I know it's really him. But what if it's not?"

It's eerily quiet for a moment. And then Mama speaks. "I. Know. My. Son." She pauses. And then, "Get out."

I hear footsteps above my head. The mudroom door closing. And the car starting. Finally, there is silence.

I have seven text messages from Cami and I can't even comprehend them. I'm sick, my whole body aches, and I lie here on the floor, unable to move. Hating Blake with all my heart. Wishing I were Gracie, asleep and oblivious.

But knowing only one thing for certain. That truly, I am Ethan Manuel De Wilde, son of Paul and Maria Quintero De Wilde, born on May 15 in Belleville, Minnesota. I live in a white house on the corner of Thirty-fifth and Maple. And nobody's going to drive me out.

I am Ethan De Wilde.

I am.

# CHAPTER 43

I wake up, drool sliding down my chin, and all my muscles ache. I'm twisted up in a blanket on the floor in my original basement spot, and it's quiet in the house for a bright Saturday morning. I wipe my mouth. My unbrushed teeth taste like cigarette ashes.

I hear a noise and look up. Mama's sitting on the edge of the pool table, watching me. Her hair is a mess and she's still wearing her clothes from last night.

"Sweetheart," she says, and then her eyes flood. "I'm so sorry."

My face screws up, and I don't want to talk about it. I don't want to be upset anymore and I don't want to remember it. "Go away," I say, softly. Gently. "Please don't look at me."

Mama brings her hand to her face and sucks in a shuddery breath. "Dad and I have no doubt that you are our son. And we're dealing with Blake. He is being severely punished. I'm so sorry—I know it hurts."

I roll over and look at the wall.

"We both love you very much. And so do Blake and Gracie."

She needs to be quiet now or I'll never believe another word she says. "Please, just go. I'll talk to you later. I can't talk about this right now."

She's quiet, and after a minute she slides off the pool table. "Okay."

Later, I hear her on the phone with the therapist, setting up another appointment. As if the weekly visits weren't wrecking things enough.

I have no thoughts. I just lie there for a long time, like I'm in a trance or something. Not feeling anything. Not knowing what to think. I hear people waking up, moving around upstairs, and I feel a buzzing in my pocket. But I don't move. I can't.

Gracie comes down when Mama's not paying attention, and I don't have the energy to send her away.

"Mama says you don't feel good today."

"Yeah," I say.

"Did you frow up?"

"No, I just feel sick."

She puts her hands on her hips and looks at me for a minute, and then turns around and runs up the steps.

I finally rouse myself enough to text Cami.

*Bad headache,* I write. *I'm sorry. Going to sleep. Talk later, k?*

*Oh no! I'm sorry for all the annoying texts. I didn't know. Feel better. Miss you.*

I doze for a while, and then I hear Gracie coming down the stairs again. I open one eye and she sets something down by my head and tiptoes back upstairs. I sit up and look at it.

It's her lunch box.

I pick it up and turn it over in my hands. And then I open it up. It's lunch. A bologna, butter, and potato chip sandwich, a granola bar, a cheese stick, and a juice box. And a folded piece of paper.

I unfold it. It's a drawing of the two of us in the living room, Gracie standing on my knees, playing elevator.

And it kills me. It really does.

I eat the lunch, and then, after a while, I hoist myself up, go into my room, and find some colored pencils, and I sketch a picture of us too. We're sitting on the sled, with matching red-and-white-striped knit caps . . . like Waldo. I fold the paper and put it into the empty lunch box, and then I leave it at the top of the steps for my sister.

. . .

And then I take a shower and get cleaned up.

Before I leave, I go upstairs and find Mama washing windows in the living room. "I'm going out for a while," I say. "I'll be back by eleven, and I have my phone on. Okay?"

Mama nods. Her eyes are rimmed red and she still looks like hell. "Will you please tell me where you're going?"

"Just over to Cami's."

"Thank you."

"Where's Dad?"

"He's around. Working in the garage."

I'm glad. I thought she might have made him leave for good when she told him to get out last night. "Okay." I turn to go, and then I hesitate. "Hey, Mama?"

She rests her arm and turns to look at me. "Yes?"

I press my lips together. "I'll take a DNA test if you want me to." My voice chokes on the words. "If that will fix things."

Mama's face grows hard. "Absolutely not."

"But why? If it'll stop all of this . . ."

"Because, Ethan." Her tone doesn't waver, but it grows softer. "Think about it. How would you feel if I say okay?"

She doesn't wait for me to answer, and I'm glad, because truth is I'd feel like shit.

"If I say okay," she says, "your whole life, you'll never forget that once, your own mother doubted you." She gives a little one-shoulder shrug and her voice is thick. "I wouldn't be able to live with that."

She touches my shoulder and makes me look her in the eye. "Hear me, son: I don't doubt you. Okay? You want to do a test for yourself, or for Blake, I won't stop you. But don't do it for me."

My eyes burn. I blink hard for a second, thinking I should say something loving, something thankful, but I can't. I try a smile, but my lips aren't working right either—it comes out crooked and quivery, but it'll have to do. And then I turn and go.

I knock on Cami's door. She opens it and flings herself into my arms. Almost knocks me off her front step. And then she's kissing me, hard, and I forget everything except how fucking in love I am. She pulls me into her house and we go downstairs to their rec room and then we're on the couch, making out, and I just hold her tight, feel her body against mine, and all I can think about is how much I want her.

I slip my hand under her shirt, tentatively, and she sucks in a breath. "My parents are upstairs," is all she says, but it's enough. I pull back and slow down. Hold her. We have plenty of time.

"I don't want to mess this up," I whisper.

"Neither do I," she says.

We both breathe and sigh, and then we laugh at our synchronicity.

We take a walk. It's thawing, some. Spring comes so late here, but it's coming. The snow along the side of the road is hideous in its old age, graying all around from dirt and exhaust.

"I hate this part of winter," Cami says. "I mean, I like that it's not so cold, but it's so ugly."

We turn down an unfamiliar street and Cami takes my hand. "You're quiet. Are you still feeling sick?"

I don't want to think about it. "Just really mellow today," I say. "Entertain me."

Cami grins. "Okay, a duck walks into a bar—" She looks sidelong at me. "Stop me if you know this one."

"I know this one," I say. I grin and tickle her. I want to tell her so much that I love her, but I can't. It's way too soon.

We spend Sunday together after church, and it's awesome being at her house, where I don't have to always be on guard for Blake. There are no fights here. Her parents are easygoing and Cami's mom is always shoving food at me, which is never a bad thing. We watch movies all together, and Cami and I snuggle up by their fireplace. It feels great to be here, like I'm on vacation or something.

But when I go home at night, it all comes flooding back. The tension in the house is heavy. And when I'm alone and I let my mind go, a little bit of doubt starts to creep in, like maybe I've gone completely batshit crazy or something. Like maybe Blake's right and I'm not really Ethan. I touch my earlobes, and they are still attached, like always. Finally, I get brave enough to look through all my remaining photos, trying to get a good view of my ears. But there are none that give me an earlobe close up enough to tell. Blake has them all.

I find out Sunday night from my little informer friend that Blake got his precious computer and iPod taken away for what he did. And Mama lets us know via a note on the table that all of us except Gracie will be going to family counseling on Wednesday after school.

"You're going to luck out again, little sister," I say. "Can I go to Grandma and Grandpa's with you instead?"

"Yeah!" she says. "They have weird snacks and Grandpa won't play elevator with me 'cause his knees are fake."

I laugh. I'd much rather play elevator than sit though another hour of hostility. "I wish I could, actually. But I can't," I say. It sucks. But maybe, eventually, the shrink will help. We can't get any worse.

# CHAPTER 44

It's so hard to look at Blake out here at the bus stop. So hard to pretend like nothing happened. I stand with Cami and we hold hands now. It's been long enough. And I'm not afraid of J-Dog anymore. Nobody can hurt me more than I've already been hurt.

I haven't told Cami what happened. I can't. I tried yesterday, but I just couldn't get the words out. Maybe it's best if nobody else ever finds out. Maybe that will make it go away.

Blake mostly looks angry. Sometimes I think he even looks a little bit sad. He doesn't look at me. Not ever. I wonder if we'll ever speak again.

I'll tell you one thing: if we do, it'll be because he's apologizing. But even then, I don't think I can ever forgive him. It feels to me like what he did was a crime, like he should go to jail for that, you know? For trying to make me into an imposter, into someone I'm not. What's the word for that, anyway? I don't think there is one.

I watch him at the bus stop, working his jaw, his eyes cold. And sometimes I think, What kind of life will we have as brothers? Will he come to my party when I graduate? Will we ever talk over waffles at the toaster again? I try to picture him and me, slapping backs and laughing about this mess later, going out to the beach with our friends and . . . whatever. I just can't see it. Will he keep everything, everyone, away from me forever because he's such a petty, jealous dickhead? Will he ever believe me?

I don't think he ever will. Sometimes, when you see someone has made up their mind about something, you know they won't even listen to reason. You see it on TV all the time, on the news, the talk shows. People sticking to their ridiculous beliefs because they made up their mind a long time ago and refuse to hear anything else, no matter how logical, no matter how thought-out, no matter how true. People get brainwashed in all sorts of ways. Not just me.

Blake is like that. He's so bitter he convinced himself he's right, and I don't think he'll ever change.

At school, I hold Cami's hand proudly and I don't

flinch when J-Dog sees us together before the bell rings. I
see his face blanch and I nod to him and keep walking to
my locker. Then I walk Cami to her first class and I kiss
her right there in front of everybody, kiss her like I love
her, like I do, and I don't care if anybody sees me or wants
to punish me for PDA or fight me for getting the best
girl in school. I'm not afraid. And I think J-Dog can tell
I'm not afraid, because he never comes to me, never talks
to me about it. And the sad thing is, he never tries to get
Cami back. If it were me, I'd sure as hell try. I guess that
shows you what kind of guy he really is.

After school, I do my homework at the kitchen table and I
eat a snack with Gracie and talk with Mama and even Dad,
when he gets home. What else am I supposed to do? When
Blake is around, I politely ignore him, because everything
between us is completely broken. It's over. I don't know
what a counselor is going to be able to do about that. But
I'll still go. I'll go because I am Ethan Manuel De Wilde,
and I am a part of this family, no matter what anybody says
or does to make me feel small. There's nothing Blake can
do now to make this worse.

    Nothing.

Still, that night, after I brush my lips against Cami's and
hold her close in the dark, cool evening, and then make

my way home to my basement and listen to the icy-cold argument in my parents' bedroom, going on and on about me again, the doubts find their way into my head. No matter how much I push them aside, it takes everything I have inside me to stop them. I lie on my stomach, arm dangling off the side of the bed, practically daring Gracie's momsters to come out from under it and snatch me away, and I can't stop thinking. Little questions slip out through the cracks of the dam I have built in my brain to keep the bad shit away. Why can't I remember anything before the abduction? Why? Was it because I wasn't really here? I can't get the nagging thoughts out of my head. This might kill me if I let it. I can't let it.

In the morning, I find Gracie's lunch box outside my bedroom door. It's been there three days in a row now. Every day there's a drawing or knickknack inside, or one of her starred or smiley-faced worksheets from school. Today it's a photo of us from my coming home party. She signed her name over it, doing cursive all totally wrong, just connecting the letters and adding curly lines around it. I take it out and slip it into my wallet. Then I put the blue race car and some marbles inside the lunch box, and leave it for her in the same spot. We don't talk about it, not to anyone or to each other. It's our own private, secret, made-up game, and we both instinctively know the rules.

• • •

After school is counseling again. And it's hard. Really, really hard. We sit there, stone-faced, refusing to talk about anything, as Dr. Frost thoughtfully taps a pencil to her lips and Mama fidgets with her purse strap, running it over and over between her thumb and forefinger, trying not to interrupt, trying to let the doc handle it. I'm sure she wants to smash our heads together, but I don't trust Blake and I'm not giving in, and neither is he, no matter how hard Mama pleads. No matter how sternly Dad stares at me.

And Dad looks at me differently now. He does. More distant. He still hugs me and says he loves me, but I know that he doubted me once. And he knows I know. That look on his face at the table when he saw Blake's photoshopped picture was a real killer. When he looks at me, I look back, focus on a point in the center of his forehead, try to let it go. It's not doing me any good.

I can't blame him. I really can't. He can't help his feelings. That's what Dr. Frost says. She says we're all okay having the feelings we have, and that what we need to do is to communicate them and work through them. That's what Dad did that night when I overheard what he said to Mama. But the bad thing about communication is that when you say something, you can't take it back. It's forever entered into memory, and you can try to dilute it all you want with opposite words, but you can't make it disappear. So no matter how many times Dad says he believes I'm his son, those words he said to Mama will always be echoing back at me.

It's okay. It is. It has to be. I think the thing that is keeping me together is what Mama did. Or rather, what she didn't do. She's convinced that I am her son, and she never doubted me. She believes in me—that's what's giving me hope right now that we'll all get through this alive. And I hang on to it. Because if you don't have at least one person believing in you, then there's not much reason to give a shit about anything.

# CHAPTER 45

At least nothing else bad happens, unless you count silence. Today with Blake looks like this: we don't acknowledge each other at breakfast, we don't look at each other at the bus stop or on the bus or anywhere. At least he stopped yelling. Though his silence is almost a little scarier than the yelling. It makes me wonder what he's up to. But I remind myself that I am new now. I'm different. I don't let him rule the way I feel anymore. I just go to school, hang out with Cami, play the lunch box game with Gracie, help my parents. Try to be normal for once, feel like a normal kid in a normal family, and it's finally working, sort of. In spite of Blake trying to wreck it all. I'm even getting decent grades. Mostly B's and C's. Not bad.

I get my first A- in English class for a paper I wrote,

and that totally makes my day, it really does. My teacher said it was compelling and it would have been an A except for some misspelled words and passive sentences. It was one of those five-paragraph personal essay assignments, and I wrote about how I found my family using the computers at the library in St. Louis. It's weird how much easier it is to write all the junk down than it is to talk about it. I show the paper to Cami on the bus ride home.

She reads it right there, holding tight to my hand. Her eyes dart back and forth. One-handed, she flips the page really fast to read the rest. "It's really good," she says.

"Thanks."

"So you were in St. Louis for almost a year, then, huh? But weren't you in the south, too?"

"Around seven years with Eleanor in Oklahoma. I guess I was there from the beginning, after the abduction, but we moved around all the time and I'm not sure about the early years." I trace my thumb along her forefinger. "Then a year in Omaha at the youth home, until I ran away from there. Hitchhiked to wherever truckers would take me after that, and I ended up homeless in St. Louis. It wasn't too bad there. I'd go back if I had to."

Cami reads over the first page again. I stare at the green seatback in front of me and ponder what I've just said. *I'd go back if I had to.* Would I? I can't imagine going back to that kind of homeless life, especially now. You're always either freezing or burning up or soaking wet, never able to get a good, deep sleep, always on the lookout for somebody to call the cops or kick you out of doorways. Always watching for people to throw stuff away, then diving after it. Smoking old cigarette butts like they're comfort food until the filter melts and your mouth tastes like burned plastic, drinking cold, bitter coffee out of people's discarded Starbucks cups.

People who don't have a clue say stupid things, like, *When things get bad enough for those people, there's no shame left.* They're wrong. There's a lot of fucking shame. It feels like total crap, living like that. Not going back there. Ever.

Cami looks up. "That was nice of the librarian to let you hang out to get warm every night."

"Yeah," I say. "Stewart. He was cool. Didn't call security on me. I just kept to myself, mostly. Sometimes he'd come up to me and make like he packed too much in his lunch, couldn't eat it all . . ." I trail off because it sounds weird to tell her I scarfed down the librarian's leftover sandwiches, kept the ziplock baggies until I was alone so I could lick out the extra peanut butter, then use the baggies to go Dumpster diving. I'm just not that guy anymore.

"I'm so glad you found that website and came home." Cami rests our entwined fingers on my thigh and leans up against me. My eyes practically roll back in my head just having her near. I'll never get over this feeling. Like I belong with someone. Like I'm finally part of something safe, something strong. Something I can count on. Like the world, the continents, really could come back together one day, the edges of land sealing up that big space of water and sky and nothingness between them.

# CHAPTER 46

It's a windy spring day. Cami and I get off the bus and start walking toward her house, as usual. "I finished my collage," I say. "Made a frame for it and everything. Maybe you can come by tonight and see it."

"Sure," she says. Her hair flies in the wind and I get a faceful of it, but I don't mind. We hang around for a minute on her front step, kissing and enjoying the warmer weather, but the clouds are building. It looks like rain. The snow is mostly gone except for the biggest piles, which have shrunk considerably and now look more like mud mounds, and the soggy yellow grass is flattened as though a steamroller went over the lawns. The snow family in my front yard is long gone.

Blake is just a fly in my life. He buzzes by now and

then, and I wave him away. At counseling the other day, we talked about one of us moving in with Grandma and Grandpa for the summer, but then we started arguing about which one of us would have to go. I know I don't want to.

The hysterics thing is getting better, it really is, thanks to Cami. She totally helps me lighten up. But it's still there sometimes when I think about things too hard and when my brain gets too full of all the crap that has happened since I came home.

I kiss Cami good-bye and jog across the yards to my house. There's an unfamiliar black sedan driving down the street slowly, with two guys in the front seat peering out the windows, like they're looking for an address. It gives me a chill when I remember Blake's account of the abduction—two guys in a black car—and it's creepy, even though I know it's ridiculous to let my mind go there.

I go inside, straight to the kitchen. Gracie is eating ice cream and she instinctively moves across the table from where I set my backpack. Never trusting me near her snacks. I grin and sit down. Mama sits down too and we talk for a minute about the day and about English class and how we're diagramming sentences, which I kind of secretly like to do.

It's starting to rain when the doorbell rings.

I look out the window. The black car from a few minutes ago is in the driveway.

"Can you answer it, hon?" Mama asks me. "I haven't sat down all day." She looks tired.

"Sure," I say. My stomach clenches.

I go to the mudroom, open the door a crack, and see them. One is short and bald, the other is taller with a mustache. "Hello?" I open the door a bit farther.

"Is this the De Wilde residence?"

I nod.

The guy with the mustache asks, "Is there a parent or guardian at home?" He flips open a badge and holds it up so I can see.

"Just a minute." I close the door and go tell Mama that the police are here.

Gracie's eyes bug out, and Mama stares at me. And then she stands and rushes to the door, whispering, "Oh my God, Paul." And suddenly I wonder if Dad was killed or something terrible like that. I follow Mama to the door, and Gracie goes to Blake's room. I can hear her high-pitched voice telling him the police are here.

Mama opens the door and invites them into the mudroom. "Can I help you?" I can hear the anxiety in her voice. She smoothes her cardigan nervously.

"Are you Maria De Wilde?"

"Yes."

The bald guy introduces himself as Detective Somebody. I don't catch the name. I'm getting light-headed.

"Would you like to sit down?" the bald guy asks Mama.

"No, thank you. What is it?" Mama asks. "Please, just tell me. Did something happen to Paul?"

The two guys exchange a quick glance, and then the bald guy says, "No, Mrs. De Wilde. We're here about your son Ethan."

My eyes open wide. Blake and Gracie are here now too, gathered in the doorway, and we're all completely silent. Gracie looks up at me. Blake's face is intense, hoping for dirt to mock me with, I'm sure.

"What about him?" Mama looks concerned now, less scared. I rack my brains, trying to think of anything I could have done wrong. Driving violations, maybe? It can't be. I've been very careful and I still only have my permit, so I'm always with Mama or Dad. I haven't done anything. I'm sure of it. But the panic grows.

"Are you sure you wouldn't like to sit down?"

"Yes, I'm sure." Instead, Mama grips the doorframe.

The bald guy nods. "Mrs. De Wilde, your son Ethan was abducted nine years ago, is that correct?"

"Yes. Did you find that woman Eleanor?"

"No, ma'am. I'm afraid we have sad news. We've found the remains of Ethan's body."

Mama's jaw drops, and for a moment it's completely silent. "What?"

"Your son is dead, ma'am. Some hikers strayed off trail up near the Canadian border and found his remains. His death . . . we believe it happened a short time after he was abducted." He pauses. "Tests confirm it's your son Ethan. I'm so sorry."

The words jump around in my head, not making sense. My stomach hurts.

Mama clutches her sweater at her throat and glances at me, then back at them. Her voice wavers. "He's not dead. You've made a mistake . . ."

"No, ma'am. I'm sorry," the detective says firmly, like he's probably had to do a hundred times. "There's no mistake. We compared DNA to the missing person's follicle sample on file—hair that was pulled from Ethan's comb back when he was abducted. Do you recall that, Mrs. De Wilde? The DNA matches."

I don't understand. I try to put the words together but my brain is cloudy and won't let it happen. So I get caught up diagramming the detective's sentences in my head like I'm sitting in English class, wondering what the hell they're doing with my comb, like maybe I dropped it when I got off the bus and they're returning it. Thinking maybe I should be grateful.

My body is so numb I can't feel my fingers. The words

repeat in my ears. Slowly the cloudiness clears.

And everything changes. The numbness goes away, and pain, like nausea, washes over me. The sentences come together, and finally . . . *finally* I understand them. I understand everything. I know where my lost memories are, the ones I've been searching for, the ones I was sure would come back someday. Racetracks and sno-cones and Rags the dog . . . and a brother I loved. All those memories are frozen, irretrievable. Buried in the wilderness under nine years of snow, nestled alongside the bones of a strange boy.

A boy named Ethan, who once had a comb, and hair that was not my hair.

I hear a ghastly moan and look around, dazed, before I realize it escaped from inside me.

As if he's just awakened from a trance, Blake turns slowly and looks at me, horrified. Scared.

Gracie doesn't understand. She tilts her head, stares. Her pink lips make a little O.

Mama's eyes meet mine. Her face crinkles and then slacks as all the color drains out of it.

Bile jumps to my throat, making me choke, cough. The dam in my brain, the one that always tries to hold back the fear and truth and insanity of my fucking life, bursts wide open and it's a flood in there. I can't hold it back, and I can't swim.

I can't breathe.

All the memories flail around—Ellen's crack-whore boyfriends beating the shit out of us. Me crying out "Mom!" and her too fucked up from drugs or fists to stop them or to help me. Running from the men, from the dealers, from the landlord, from the cops. And her getting rid of me. That's what messed me up the worst. After all of that, she dumped me off and never came back. Real mothers wouldn't do that.

Would they?

How could they?

I wonder, when was the first time I thought about it . . . wished for it? Was it tiny at first? So tiny, maybe, that it was barely even a complete thought. It hummed to me. *Maybe I have a different family somewhere.* I remember it now. On the freezing-cold nights, it gave me something to stay alive for. God, I wanted it so bad. The library, the searches. And then, bam! There, on the screen in front of me. Like looking in a mirror. Every day I stared at that picture, every day I read a little bit more, thinking maybe. Maybe.

Maybe.

Imagining it. The more I learned about the boy, the more uncertain I was about my past. The more convinced I became. This was it.

I was so sure.

And now . . . here in the mudroom, it's all crashing down and I'm drowning in it.

Ethan is dead.

I am nothing. Nameless. No one.

I gasp for air.

When Mama cries out, I hear months, years, of grief in her voice. Her sweet, dark eyes and little round body, her fingers that slip off the doorframe and clutch at her throat, just like the first time I saw her, her faltering knees that threaten to buckle.

I turn away, lean hard against the wall, feeling my gut seize up, the boot kicking my ribs and stopping my breath, and then I push against the service door to the garage as if the wood, the brass handle, can give me strength to face them. To face these people, this family surrounding me . . . as they begin breaking to pieces all over again.

I glance at Gracie as she starts to point at me, and I imagine what she's about to say to the police, to Mama.

*That's Efan right there*, she'll explain, all innocent and beautiful. Then she'll smile proudly like she solved the puzzle.

And they'll have to tell her, after.

And Cami . . . oh God. The boot kicks so hard my ribs crack. My body tenses and wants to crack too.

It's not fair. It isn't. Not to Mama, or any of them. Not to me.

As time speeds up again, I open the door and take one last look over my shoulder at the devastation I created. At my sweet Gracie . . . My heart rips. And at Blake, who will finally be right. And then I look at the detectives, imagining the scene when it all spills out. That old, familiar panic wells up.

Mama falls.

They catch her.

And I run.

# crash

My sophomore psych teacher, Mr. Polselli, says knowledge is crucial to understanding the workings of the human brain, but I swear to dog, I don't want any more knowledge about this.

Every few days I see it. Sometimes it's just a picture, like on that billboard we pass on the way to school. And other times it's moving, like on a screen. A careening truck hits a building and explodes. Then nine body bags in the snow.

It's like a movie trailer with no sound, no credits. And nobody sees it but me.

Some days after psych class I hang around by the door of Mr. Polselli's room for a minute, thinking that if I have a mental illness, he's the one who'll be able to tell me. But every time I almost mention it, it sounds too weird to say. *So, uh, Mr. Polselli, when other people see the "turn off your cell phones" screen in the movie theater, I see an extra five-second movie trailer. Er . . . and did I mention I see stills of it on the billboard by my house? You see Jose Cuervo, I see a truck hitting a building and everything exploding. Is that normal?*

The first time was in the theater on the one holiday that our parents don't make us work—Christmas Day. I poked my younger sister, Rowan. "Did you see that?"

She did this eyebrow thing that basically says she thinks I'm an idiot. "See what?"

"The explosion," I said softly.

"You're on drugs." Rowan turned to our older brother, Trey, and said, "Jules is on drugs."

Trey leaned over Rowan to look at me. "Don't do drugs," he said seriously. "Our family has enough problems."

I rolled my eyes and sat back in my seat as the real movie trailers started. "No kidding," I muttered. And I reasoned with myself. The day before I'd almost been robbed while doing a pizza delivery. Maybe I was still traumatized.

I just wanted to forget about it all.

But then on MLK Day this stupid vision thing decided to get personal.


Five reasons why I, Jules Demarco, am shunned:
1. I smell like pizza
2. My parents make us drive a meatball-topped food
   truck to school for advertising

3. I haven't invited a friend over since second grade
4. Did I mention I smell like pizza? Like, its umami*-
   ness oozes from my pores
5. Everybody at school likes Sawyer Angotti's
   family's restaurant better

Frankly, I don't blame them. I'd shun me too.

Every January my mother says Martin Luther King Jr. weekend
gives us the boost we need to pay the rent after the first two dead
weeks of the year. She's superpositive about everything. It's like
she forgets that every month is the same. Her attitude is probably what keeps our business alive. But if my mother, Paula, is
the backbone of Demarco's Pizzeria, my father, Antonio, is the
broken leg that keeps us struggling to catch up.

There's no school on MLK Day, so Trey and I are manning
the meatball truck in downtown Chicago, and Rowan is working
front of house in the restaurant for the lunch shift. She's jealous.
But Trey and I are the oldest, so we get to decide.

The food truck is actually kind of a blast, even if it does have
two giant balls on top, with endless jokes to be made. Trey and I
have been cooking together since we were little—he's only sixteen
months older than me. He's a senior. He's supposed to be the one
driving the food truck to school because he has his truck license
now, but he pays me ten bucks a week to secretly drive it so he can

---

*look it up

bum a ride from our neighbor Carter. Carter is kind of a douche, but at least his piece-of-crap Buick doesn't have a sack on its roof.

Trey drives now and we pass the billboard again.

"Hey—what was on the billboard?" I ask as nonchalantly as I can.

Trey narrows his eyes and glances at me. "Same as always. Jose Cuervo. Why?"

"Oh." I shrug like it's no big deal. "Out of the corner of my eye I thought it had changed to something new for once." Weak answer, but he accepts it. To me, the billboard is a still picture of the explosion. I look away and rub my temples as if it will make me see what everybody else sees, but it does nothing. Instead, I try to forget by focusing on my phone. I start posting all over the Internet where Demarco's Food Truck is going to be today. I'm sure some of our regulars will show up. It's becoming a sport, like storm chasing. Only they're giant meatball chasing.

Some people need a life. Including me.

We roll past Angotti's Trattoria on the way into the city— that's Sawyer's family's restaurant. Sawyer is working today too. He's outside sweeping the snow from their sidewalk. I beg for the traffic light to stay green so we can breeze past unnoticed, but it turns yellow and Trey slows the vehicle. "You could've made it," I mutter.

Trey looks at me while we sit. "What's your rush?"

I glance out the window at Sawyer, who either hasn't noticed our obnoxious food truck or is choosing to ignore it.

Trey follows my glance. "Oh," he says. "The enemy. Let's wave!"

I shrink down and pull my hat halfway over my eyes. "Just . . . hurry," I say, even though there's nothing Trey can do. Sawyer turns around to pick up a bag of rock salt for the ice, and I can tell he catches sight of our truck. His head turns slightly so he can spy on who's driving, and then he frowns.

Trey nods coolly at Sawyer when their eyes meet, and then he faces forward as the light finally changes to green. "Do you still like him?" he asks.

Here's me, sunk down in the seat like a total loser, trying to hide, breathing a sigh of relief when we start rolling again. "Yeah," I say, totally miserable. "Do you?"

Trey smiles. "Nah. That urban underground thing he's got going on is nice, and of course I'm fond of the, ah, Mediterranean complexion, but I've been over him for a while. He's too young for me. You can have him."

I laugh. "Yeah, right. Dad will love that. Maybe me hooking up with an Angotti will be the thing that puts him over the edge." I don't mention that Sawyer won't even look at me these days, so the chance of me "having" Sawyer is zero.

Sawyer Angotti is not the kind of guy most people would say is hot, but Trey and I have the same taste in men, which is sometimes convenient and sometimes a pain in the ass. Sawyer has this street casual look where he could totally be a clothes model, but if he ever told people he was one, they'd be like, "Seriously? No way." Because his most attractive features are so subtle, you know? At first glance he's really ordinary, but if you study him . . . big sigh. His vulnerable smile is what gets me—not the charming one he uses on teachers and girls and probably customers, too. I mean the warm, crooked smile that doesn't come out unless he's feeling shy or self-conscious. That one makes my stomach flip. Because for the most part, he's tough-guy metro, if such a thing exists. Arms crossed and eyebrow raised, constantly questioning the world. But I've seen his other side a million times. I've been in love with him since we played plastic cheetahs and bears together at indoor recess in first grade.

How was I supposed to know back then that Sawyer was the enemy? I didn't even know his last name. And I didn't know about the family rivalry. But the way my father interrogated me after they went to my first parent-teacher conference and found out that I "played well with others" and "had a nice friend in Sawyer Angotti," you'd have thought I'd given away great-grandfather's last weapon to the enemy. Trey says that was right around the time Dad really started acting weird.

All I knew was that I wasn't allowed to play cheetahs and bears with Sawyer anymore. I wasn't even supposed to talk to him.

But I still did, and he still did, and we would meet under the slide and trade suckers from the candy jar each of our restaurants had by the cash register. I would bring him grape, and he always brought me butterscotch, which we never had in our restaurant.

I'd do anything to get Sawyer Angotti to give me a butterscotch sucker again.

I have a notebook from sixth grade that has nine pages filled with embarrassing and overdramatic phrases like "I pine for Sawyer Angotti" and "JuleSawyer forever." I even made an S logo for our conjoined names in that one. Too bad it looks more like a cross between a dollar sign and an ampersand. I'd dream about us getting secretly married and never telling our parents.

And back then I'd moon around in my room after Rowan was asleep, pretending my pillow was Sawyer. Me and my Sawyer pillow would lie down on my bed, facing one another, and I'd imagine us in Bulger Park on a blanket, ignoring the tree frogs and pigeons and little crying kids. I'd touch his cheek and push his hair back, and he'd look at me with his gorgeous green eyes and that crooked, shy grin of his, and then he'd lean toward me and we'd both hold our breath without realizing it, and his lips would touch mine, and then . . . He'd be my first kiss, which I'd never forget. And no matter how much our parents tried to keep us apart, he'd never break my heart.

Oh, sigh.

But then, on the day before seventh grade started, when it was time to visit school to check out classes and get our books, his father was there with him, and my father was there with me, and I did something terrible.

Without thinking, I smiled and waved at my friend, and he smiled back, and I bit my lip because of love and delight after not seeing him for the whole summer . . . and his father saw me. He frowned, looked up at my father, scowled, and then grabbed Sawyer's arm and pulled him away, giving my father one last heated glance. My father grumbled all the way home, issuing half-sentence threats under his breath.

And that was the end of that.

I don't know what his father said or did to him that day, but by the next day, Sawyer Angotti was no longer my friend. Whoever said seventh grade is the worst year of your life was right. Sawyer turned our friendship off like a faucet, but I can't help it—my faucet of love has a really bad leak.

Trey parks the truck as close to the Field Museum as our permit allows, figuring since the weather is actually sunny and not too freezing and windy, people might prefer to grab a quick meal from a food truck instead of eating the overpriced generic stuff inside the tourist trap.

Before we open the window for business, we set up. Trey checks the meat sauce while I grate fresh mozzarella into tiny, easily meltable nubs. It's a simple operation—our winter truck specialty is an Italian bread bowl with spicy mini meatballs, sauce, and cheese. The truth is it's delicious, even though I'm sick to death of them.

We also serve our pizza by the slice, and we're talking deep-dish Chicago-style, not that thin crap that Angotti's serves. Authentic, authschmentic. The tourists want the hearty, crusty, saucy stuff with slices of sausage the diameter of my bicep and bubbling cheese that stretches the length of your forearm. That's what we've got, and it's amazing.

Oh, but the Angotti's sauce . . . I had it once, even though in our house it's contraband. Their sauce will lay you flat, seriously. It's that good. We even have the recipe, apparently, but we can't use it because it's patented and they sell it by the jar—it's in all the local stores and some regional ones now too. My dad about had an aneurysm when that happened. Because, according to Dad, in one of his mumble-grumble fits, the Angottis had been after our recipe for generations and somehow managed to steal it from us.

So I guess that's how the whole rivalry started. From what I understand, and from what I know about Sawyer avoiding me like the plague, his parents feel the same way about us as my parents feel about them.

Trey and I pull off a really decent day of sales for the middle of January. We hightail it back home for the dinner rush so we can help Rowan out.

As we get close, we pass the billboard from the other side. I locate it in my side mirror, and it's the same as this morning. Explosion. I watch it grow small and disappear, and then close my eyes, wondering what the hell is wrong with me.

We pull into the alley and park the truck, take the stuff inside.

"Get your asses out there!" Rowan hisses as she flies through the kitchen. She gets a little anxious when people have to wait ten seconds. That kid is extremely well put together, but she carries the responsibility of practically the whole country on her shoulders.

Mom is rolling out dough. I give her a kiss on the cheek and shake the bank bag in her face to show her I'm on the way to putting it in the safe like I'm supposed to. "Pretty good day. Had a busload of twenty-four," I say.

"Fabulous!" Mom says, way too perky. She grabs a tasting utensil, reaches into a nearby pot, and forks a meatball for me. I let her shove it into my mouth when I pass her again.

"I's goo'!" I say. And really freaking hot. It burns the roof of my mouth before I can shift it between my teeth to let it cool.

Tony, the cook who has been working for our family restaurant for something like forty million years, smiles at me. "Nice work today, Julia," he says. Tony is one of the few people I allow to call me by my birth name.

I guess my dad, Antonio, was actually named after Tony. Tony and my grandfather came to America together. I don't really remember my grandpa much—he killed himself when I was little. Depression. A couple of years ago I accidentally found out it was suicide when I overheard Mom and Aunt Mary talking about it.

When I asked my mom about it later, she didn't deny it—instead, she said, "But you kids don't have any sign of depression in you, so don't worry. You're all fine." Which was about the best way to make me think I'm doomed.

It's a weird thing to find out about your family, you know? It made me feel really different for the rest of the day, and it still does now whenever I think about it. Like we're all wondering where the depression poison will hit next, and we're all looking at my dad. I wonder if that's why my mother is so upbeat all the time. Maybe she thinks she can protect us with her happy shield.

Trey and I hurry to wash up, grab fresh aprons, and check in with Aunt Mary at the hostess stand. She's seating somebody, so we take a look at the chart and see that the house is pretty full. No wonder Rowan's freaking out.

Rowan's fifteen and a freshman. Just as Trey is sixteen months older than me, she's sixteen months younger. I don't know if my parents planned it, and I don't want to know, but there it is. I pretty much think they had us for the sole purpose of working for the family business. We started washing dishes and busing tables years ago. I'm not sure if it was legal, but it was definitely tradition.

Rowan looks relieved to see us. She's got the place under control, as usual. "Hey, baby! Go take a break," I whisper to her in passing.

"Nah, I'm good. I'll finish out my tables," she says. I glance at the clock. Technically, Rowan is supposed to quit at seven, because she's not sixteen yet—she can only work late in the summer—but, well, tradition trumps rules sometimes. Not that my parents are slave drivers or anything. They're not. This is just their life, and it's all they know.

It's a busy night because of the holiday. Busy is good. Busy means we can pay the rent, and whatever else comes up. Something always does.

By ten thirty all the customers have left. Even though Dad hasn't come down at all this evening to help out, Mom says she and Tony can handle closing up alone, and she sends Trey and me upstairs to the apartment to get some sleep.

I don't want to go up there.

Neither does Trey.

Trey and I go out the back and into the door to the stairs leading up to our home above the restaurant. We pick our way up the stairs, through the narrow aisle that isn't piled with stuff. At the top, we push against the door and squeeze through the space.

Rowan has already done what she could with the kitchen. The sink is empty, the counters are clean. The kitchen is the one sacred spot, the one room where Mom won't take any garbage from anybody—literally. Because even after cooking all day, she still likes to be able to cook at home too, without having to worry that Dad's precious stacks of papers are going to combust and set the whole building on fire because they're too close to the gas stove.

Everywhere else—dining room, living room, and hallway—is piled high around the edges with Dad's stuff. Lots of papers—recipes and hundreds of cooking magazines, mostly, and all the Chicago newspapers from the past decade. Shoe boxes, shirt boxes, and every other possible kind of box you can imagine, some filled with papers, some empty. Plastic milk crates filled with cookbooks and science books and gastronomy magazines. Bags full of greeting cards, birthday cards, sympathy cards, some written in, some brand-new, meant for good intentions that never happened. Hundreds of old videos, and a stack as high as my collarbone of old VCRs that don't work. Stereos, 8-track players, record players, tape recorders, all broken. Records and cassette tapes and CDs and games—oh my dog, the board games. Monopoly, Life, Password, Catch Phrase. Sometimes five or six duplicates, most of them with little yellowing masking-tape stickers on them that say seventy-five cents or a buck twenty-five. Insanity. Especially when somebody puts something heavy on top of a Catch Phrase and that stupid beeper goes off somewhere far below, all muffled.

We weave through it. Thankfully, Dad is nowhere to be found, either asleep or buried alive under all his crap. It's not like he's violent or mean or anything. He's just . . . unpredictable. When he's feeling good, he's in the restaurant. He's visible. He's easy to keep track of. But on the days he doesn't come down, we never know what to expect. We climb those stairs after the end of our shift knowing he could be standing right there in the kitchen, long-faced, unshaven, having surfaced to eat something for the first time since yesterday. And rattling off the same guilt-inspired apologies, day after day after day. *I just couldn't make it down today. Not feeling up to it. I'm sorry you kids have to work so hard.* What do you say to that after the tenth time, or the hundredth?

Worse, he could be sitting in the dark living room with his hands covering his face, the blue glow from the muted TV spotlighting his depressed existence so we can't ignore it. It's probably wrong that Trey and Rowan and I all hope he stays invisible, holed up in his bedroom on days like these, but it's just easier when he's out of sight. We can pretend depressed Dad doesn't exist.

Tonight we breathe a sigh of relief. Trey heads into the cluttered bathroom, its cupboards overflowing with enough soap, shampoo, toothpaste, and toilet paper to get us through Y3K. Thank God our bedrooms are off-limits to Dad. I peek into my tidy little room and see Rowan is sleeping in her bed already, but I'm still wired from a long day. I close the door quietly and grab a glass of milk from the kitchen, then settle down in the one chair in the living room that's not full of stuff and flip on the TV. I run through the DVR list, choosing a rerun of an old Sherlock Holmes movie that I've been watching a little bit at a time over the past couple of weeks, whenever I get a chance. Somebody else must be watching it too, because it's not cued up to the last part I watched. I hit the slowest fast-forward so I can find where I left off.

Trey peeks his head in the room. "Night," he says. He dangles the keys to the meatball truck, and when I hold out my hand, he tosses them to me.

"Thanks," I say, not meaning it. I shouldn't have agreed to only ten bucks a week, but I was desperate. It's not nearly enough to pay for the humiliation of driving the giant balls. "Where's my ten bucks?"

"Isn't it only eight if one day is a holiday?" He gives me what he thinks is his adorable face and hands me a five and three ones.

"Sorry. Not in the contract." I hold my hand out for more.

"Dammit." He goes back to his room for two more dollars while Sir Henry on the TV is flitting around outside on the moors in fast mode, which looks kind of kooky.

Trey returns. "Here."

I grab the two bucks from him and shove all ten into my pocket with my tips. "Thanks. Night."

When he's gone, I stop the fast-forward, knowing I went too far, and rewind to the commercial as I slip the keys into my other pocket, then press play.

Instead of the movie that I'm expecting, I see *it* again.

It flashes by in a few seconds, and then it's gone. The truck, the building, the explosion. And then back to our regularly scheduled programming.

"Stop it," I whisper. My stomach flips and a creepy shiver runs down my neck. It makes my throat tighten. I pause the recording and sit there a minute, trying to calm down. And then I hit rewind.

Ninety-nine percent of me hopes there's nothing there but a creepy giant hound on the moor.

But there it is.

I watch it again, and I get this gnawing thing in my chest, like I'm supposed to do something about it.

"Why does this keep happening?" I mutter, and rewind it again. I hit play and it all flies by so fast, I can hardly see it. I rewind once more and this time set it to play in slow motion.

The truck is yellow. I notice it's actually a snowplow, and the snow is falling pretty hard. It's dark outside, but the streetlamps are lit. The truck is coming fast and it starts angling slightly, crossing to the wrong side and going off the road. It jumps the curb spastically and jounces over some snow piles in a big parking lot, and then I see the building—there's a large window—for a split second before the truck hits it. The building explodes shortly after contact, glass and brick shrapnel flying everywhere. The scene cuts to the body bags in the snow. I count again to make sure—definitely nine. The last frame is a close-up of three of the bags, and then it's over. I hit the pause button.

"What are you doing?"

I jump and whirl around to see Rowan standing in the doorway squinting at me, hair all disheveled. "Jeez!" I whisper, trying to calm my heartbeat. "You scared the crap out of me." I glance back at the TV with slow-motion dread, like I've just been caught looking at . . . I don't know. Porn, or something else I'm not supposed to look at. But it's paused at a sour cream commercial. I let out a breath of relief and turn my attention back to Rowan.

She shrugs. "Sorry. I thought I heard Mom come up."

"Not yet. Not for a while."

She scratches her head, the sleeve of her boy jammies wagging against her cheek. "You coming to bed soon? Or do you want me to stay up with you?"

Her sweet, sleepy disposition is one of my favorites, maybe because she can be so mellow and generous when she just wakes up. I suck in my bottom lip, thinking, and look at the remote control in my hand. "Nah, I'm coming to bed now. Just gotta brush my teeth."

She scrunches up her face and yawns. "What time is it?"

I laugh softly. "Around eleven, I guess. Eleven fifteen."

"Okay," she says, turning to go back down the hallway to our bedroom. "Night."

I look at the TV once more and close my weary eyes for a moment. Then I turn it off and stand up, setting the remote on top of the set so it doesn't get buried, and carefully pick my way to the bathroom, and on to bed. But I don't think I'll be sleeping anytime soon.